THE BAKER'S BEAUTY

THE RIVER HILL SERIES

REBECCA NORINNE

JAMAILA BRINKLEY

ABOUT THIS BOOK

Say hello to River Hill, where life is a little bit sweet, and a whole lotta spicy.

After tragedy struck, Sean Amory left L.A. to come home to River Hill and work in his family's bakery. The familiar surroundings soothe his raw nerves while the gorgeous brunette who jogs past every morning has another effect entirely. And when Jess helps him out of a bind, he learns she's even sweeter than the apple fritters he's become famous for.

Former beauty queen Jessica Casillas-Moore hasn't eaten carbs since she was fourteen, but that doesn't stop her from jogging past The Breadery every morning. And when she meets the handsome baker who works there, Sean is every bit as mouthwatering as the pastries he serves. And so much better for her waistline.

But between her family's disapproval and his haunting past,

the odds seem stacked against them. Can Sean and Jess learn to trust in each other and their growing love, or is their relationship a recipe for disaster?

"I don't know much about interventions, but I think you're doing it wrong." Sean Amory peered over the rim of his glass at his friends. "For starters, I'm pretty sure you're not supposed to do it at a bar."

Max Vergaras rested his elbow on the sticky surface of The Hut's bar top, making a face as his shirt moved in a different direction than his skin. "It's the only place we can find you these days."

"It's here or work," Noah Bradstone added, taking a seat on the other side of Sean as Iain Brennan nodded in agreement from behind him.

"So?" Sean sipped his whiskey, ignoring the concern written all over their faces. "Disappointed I'm not drinking yours?" He aimed the barb at Iain.

"We don't distribute here. Just Frankie's," the Irishman answered with an easy shrug.

"I don't drink at Frankie's."

"Not anymore, you don't," Max said. He owned Frankie's, and when he wasn't in the kitchen, he was behind the bar. He had a fair idea of how much his customers drank on any given night, which was precisely why Sean had stopped drinking there.

"I didn't know you were hurting for business."

Max rolled his eyes but didn't bother to respond. Frankie's—and many of the other businesses that rounded out River Hill's ridiculously charming downtown—had never been better. Some recent high profile publicity for the town had brought the tourists in droves, and everyone appreciated the extra income, if not the actual vacationers.

Noah leaned in. "Sean, you know why we're here."

"Slumming?" Noah's highbrow wine labels weren't available at The Hut any more than Iain's fancy whiskey was.

"You need help." Noah's thick eyebrows snapped down into a frown. "Seriously."

"I'm fine."

"You're drinking too much."

"Maybe you're not drinking enough." These men had been his friends for years. Iain was new to the pack, having moved to River Hill to cohabit with the notoriously prickly Naomi Klein last year, but the others knew him well. Right now, though, Sean wished he'd never met them.

"Listen." Noah was taking the lead again. Sean briefly imagined slamming his friend's head into the ancient bar top in front of them, then shook his head slightly to clear it. Violence wasn't his style. Did the guys have a point? He transferred his glare from the group to the glass in front of him as Noah continued speaking. "My therapist is always saying to think about what it would *look* like if you confronted the things you're running from, if your worst fears came true. Then—"

He snorted a bitter laugh. "That's the last thing I need to imagine."

He knew *exactly* what it would look like. Cal Grissom's too-pale face, slack in death, had been floating into his vision every time he closed his eyes for the last year and a half. Drinking was the only thing that blurred the grisly image, the only thing that stopped him waking up in the middle of the night reaching helplessly toward the kid's hand, dangling loosely over the side of the perfectly made-up hotel room bed, still clutching the pill bottle that had killed him. Rigor mortis had made his fingers curve to the shape of the bottle even after they'd pried it out, a detail Sean wished every single day he could forget.

"I think you should call a therapist. If not mine, then a different one." Noah reached out and plucked the half-empty glass from Sean's loose grip. "This isn't cutting it, my friend." He sniffed the glass. "I'm pretty sure Johnnie Walker's degree is strictly honorary."

"Fuck you." He'd meant for the insult to be biting, but it just came out sounding tired. He didn't try to get the glass back.

Max sighed. "Whether you decide to call a shrink or not, brother, this phase is over. We're calling it."

"What are you talking about?"

The chef exchanged a nod with the bartender, who shot Sean a guilty glance. "Sorry, Sean. Big Mitch called a few minutes ago. You're cut off."

"What?" This was the last thing he'd expected. Nagging him to get help he could deal with. Bringing Big Mitch into the picture was a little extreme. The head of River Hill's resident biker gang was a silent owner of The Hut, a fact not many people knew. Except the other small business owners of River Hill, of course. "What the hell did you do?" he said, turning on Max.

Iain laid a hand on Sean's back, warm through the fabric

of his vintage tee. "Sorry, lad. It's done. I'm afraid you won't be served at any bar in town."

"You ..." Sean seethed. He couldn't even get words out.

"It's for your own good," Max said. "You'll thank us later. Maybe."

"I don't give a shit whether you thank us or not," Noah added. "I just want you upright and alive by the end of the year, and this is the only way we could see to make that happen."

"I'll just go out of town to drink, then." Sean rolled his eyes. "Your perfect plan has some pretty big holes in it, guys."

"Well, that's your choice," Noah said. "But I have to tell you this particular plan was Plan B."

"What was Plan A?" Did he even want to know?

Noah sighed. "Angelica just got a seat on the tourism board. With your mom." Noah's girlfriend was a former actress who'd opened a bed and breakfast in River Hill last year, leveraging her former career to get a deal with a TV network to film the renovation. The show had brought a lot of good publicity to River Hill, and pretty much everybody adored her these days. Including Sean's mother, who owned the family bakery. Where he now worked.

The only thing he did these days besides drink, and the only thing that had given him a lifeline when it had felt like his entire world had spun out of control, was head to the bakery. He'd come home to River Hill to work, hoping the familiar actions of kneading, cutting, and baking would soothe his bruised soul after what had happened in L.A.

But his mother didn't know about the drinking part, as far as he knew.

"I hate your girlfriend," he told Noah. "And you can tell her I said so."

"You can tell her yourself if you do it sober," Noah said. "And she told me to tell *you* that."

* * *

SEAN SHOOK the bleariness of sobriety out of his eyes as he bent over a sheet of scone dough. His head was aching more than it usually did on the days he was hungover.

He sliced mechanically through the thick dough on a diagonal with his bench scraper, the movement economical as only years of practice could make it. He might have spent the last ten years in L.A. working his way up the ladder as a record producer, but he'd grown up doing this. Baking was in his bones. The Amory family had owned The Breadery since River Hill had been founded.

He slid the scones onto a waiting sheet pan and popped them into the huge oven, pulling out two oversized muffin tins before he closed the door. He prodded the muffins with a finger, then spun the tins onto the counter to cool enough that he could turn out the goodies inside and put them into the display case before opening. Which he wasn't looking forward to.

It was the quiet mornings alone in the bakery that had brought him back here. Sometimes, he thought the bakery had saved his life. He'd been shell-shocked, shattered after finding his protégé dead. Producing records had suddenly seemed like an incredible waste of time. A week after he'd buried the kid, Sean had returned to the one thing he knew he could do productively: feeding people. When he'd asked for the opening shift, the bakery's other employees had practically thrown him a party. His mother hadn't asked any questions either. She'd simply handed over the keys and a couple of quick instructions he hadn't really needed.

It turned out baking was like riding a bike. You never really forgot how, especially when every turn of the dough, every shake of the sifter, and every sprinkle of cinnamon brought color back into your pale, dry life.

But he still hadn't been able to shake the nightmares. So he'd been drinking. Maybe his friends were right, though, and it was too much.

Today was the first morning in ages he hadn't merely gone through the motions of mixing, scooping, rolling, and flipping. The line of pastries already in the display case shone softly in the light, sugar crystals winking slightly. Sean sighed and rested his head against the side of the huge refrigerator.

Sobriety might be healthy, but it was hard as shit. He wanted a drink.

Instead, he swept the used parchment paper and crumbs lining the countertop into a trash bag and spun it swiftly to bring the ends together. He tied a knot in the top and hooked a finger through it, lifting the bag and taking it to the back door toward the dumpster, which was cleverly disguised behind a faux picket fence. Because this was River Hill, and everything was relentlessly pretty here. Even the dumpsters.

Sean heaved the bag over the edge of the fence, then paused to admire the sunrise for a brief moment before going back inside to start on his next batch of danishes. Picket fences, window boxes full to bursting with color, and delicate filigree gazebos were one thing; this was real beauty.

The Breadery opened at seven in the morning for folks who wanted a quick breakfast pastry to go with their coffee from The Hollow Bean across the town square. That meant he arrived no later than four to prepare the morning's offerings. A few doughs got made by whoever closed the night before—usually his mom and one of the other employees—but the quick breads and all the decorative work had to get done before the sun came up.

He stretched, feeling his back crack, then paused as he heard an unexpected sound. Was that somebody running?

His body came alert without conscious thought, years of living in L.A. taking his mind into danger mode immediately. He wasn't about to deal with another tragedy, especially not here on his home turf. Just the thought of seeing another dead body here, in his safe haven, made his blood boil. He turned, ready to do something—although he wasn't entirely sure what—and saw the source of the running footsteps.

It was only a jogger. His body sagged, then straightened as he got a closer look. She was toned and lean, but with just enough curves in all the right places. Tanned skin wrapped in black compression leggings and a purple tank that left the lines of her shoulders bare to the thin morning light. Long dark hair, swept back into a thick ponytail, swung with every rhythmic step. She slowed as she came closer to the bakery, and he stepped back, not wanting to get in her way. His back hit the doorframe, and he watched, enraptured, as she slowed to a walk. The woman took deep breaths, lifting her head and closing her eyes. It seemed like she was sniffing the air. Then again, perhaps she was. He was mostly used to it, but the heady scents coming from the ovens were most potent at this time of day.

His foot scuffed the ground, and her eyes flew open. When she saw him staring, he felt himself blushing like a teenager. It was like she'd caught him peeping. He raised a hand awkwardly, and she smiled at him, then sped past without a word. A few long steps later, she was gone, jogging around the corner and into the foot traffic of a River Hill morning.

Sean let out a breath he hadn't noticed he was holding. Well, *that* was something new. If he saw beauty like that every time he took a break in the morning, he'd come out to admire the sunrise a hell of a lot more often.

As it was, this was the first morning he'd taken even a

moment out of the simple routine he'd clung to as a lifeline when he came home. And to be honest, it was the first morning in months he'd been sober enough to appreciate anything anyhow. Had she been there all along?

What else had he been missing?

CHAPTER 2

Jessica Casillas-Moore sagged through her front door. Bent over at the waist, she took a few deep breaths before straightening. She raised her arm and tapped the screen on her digital watch to gauge her progress. Three miles. Not bad. Not great either, but some days getting out of bed for a pre-dawn run was harder than others. If she were being honest with herself, that was the case more often than not these days.

Fanning the long, chocolate brown hair off the back of her neck as she made her way to the bathroom at the back of her tiny cottage, Jess wondered if it was time to reconsider her priorities in life. She'd won a few pageants when she was younger, and she'd managed to leverage her so-called 'beauty queen' status into both a successful beauty blog and, most recently, a job as a lifestyle 'guru' for a few local TV stations. But she couldn't remember the last time she'd enjoyed a meal with friends or family without counting the calories of everything she consumed. She had friends who swore by skinny margaritas and oven-baked tortilla chips, but as far as

Jess was concerned, she'd rather have the real thing or nothing at all.

Which brought to mind the route she'd traversed this morning. After attending her niece's birthday party a handful of weeks ago and not eating any of the prettily-decorated cupcakes or cookies from The Breadery, River Hill's famous bakery, she'd taken to running past there every morning instead. If she couldn't *eat* any of their baked goods, Jess reasoned inhaling the sweet, buttery scent was close to the next best thing. Although after the handsome—if slightly bleary-eyed—baker had caught her sniffing the air this morning, she might have to reconsider that plan.

Now, Jess peeled the sweaty athletic gear from her body and stood naked in front of the mirror on her closet door, turning this way and that to inspect her reflection. Even with constant diet and exercise, some of her natural curves were a bit softer than they'd once been, and her breasts didn't sit quite so high up as they had even a year ago. She cupped them and then dropped her hands away, watching the weighty flesh bounce and then settle back into place.

She'd always heard a woman's body changed drastically once she hit thirty, and with that date looming in the not-too-distant future, Jess wondered what other changes she could expect. She turned and stared back over her shoulder at her rear, surveying it for any new signs of cellulite. Between the fifteen miles she ran each week and the squats and lunges her trainer made her do three times a week, it was arguably her best feature. Even so, as someone whose professional longevity was tied to her beauty, she knew all too well that age and gravity waited for no woman.

With a weary sigh, she turned on the hot water and waited for the bathroom to steam up. Grabbing a new razor from a basket under the sink, she stepped into the shower while giving herself a pep talk. It was no use getting depressed before brunch with her family. Her two older brothers—with their constant nagging about when she was finally going to settle down and start having babies—could be counted on to darken her mood all by themselves.

* * *

"Eat up, mija." Celia Casillas, Jessica's abuela, patted her shoulder as she made her way to the stove. "You're too skinny. Men like a woman with meat on her bones."

"If I eat any of this," Jess said, gesturing to the chips, salsa, and guacamole spread out on the kitchen table in front of her, "I won't have room for your albondigas or papa's tri-tip."

"And we know how much Jess likes her balls," her sister Marisol cackled as she grabbed three Coronas from the refrigerator on her way through the kitchen to join their brothers Robert and Manny in the backyard.

"Not as much as you love *your* meat," Jess replied through a pasted-on grin as the screen door clanged shut. She loved her siblings, but as the youngest of four, she'd been the butt of their jokes her whole damn life. As a kid, she'd assumed they'd all grow out of it, but she hadn't been that lucky.

Jess's grandmother set a beer down in front of her. "Ignore her. She's just trying to get under your skin."

"Well, she's doing a pretty good job of it. She knows it's inappropriate to talk like that in front of you. Heck, in front of anyone."

"You know your sister. She likes to shock people." Her grandma settled into the chair across from Jess and loaded a tortilla chip up with homemade salsa. She brought it to her mouth but halted just before taking a bite. "She's jealous, you know?"

Jess snorted and shook her head. "No way. She thinks I'm pathetic." That was one of the things that hurt the most about her relationship with her siblings. Jess had worked hard for years to get where she was—first with beauty pageants, and then with building her own consulting business, and now her YouTube channel, blog, and stints as a lifestyle expert on local news and radio shows.

She'd worked full time while putting herself through school, and while she might not have a life that mirrored the rest of her family's, she'd built something to be proud of. She had made a name for herself, but lately, it seemed like the only time anyone cared was when she could get them free stuff. Otherwise, all they ever did was tease her about her diet, her makeup, or the lack of a man in her life.

The first two she could handle. Jess knew she'd chosen a career path that some might consider shallow, but the constant jibes about her thinking she was too good for any of the men they introduced her to were low blows. She wasn't arrogant or stuck-up; she was *discerning*. Why that was a bad thing, she didn't know. With the divorce rate so high in her extended family, she would have thought they'd applaud her for not settling for less than she deserved. Instead, her brothers and sister used her single status to mock her. It wasn't like she *liked* going home to an empty house each night.

Chewing around her food, her grandma said, "No, mija. She spends her days carting the boys to and from school and then going to PTA meetings and practices, and now she wishes she'd made different choices when she was younger. I love Marisol—and I would kill for my grandbabies—but she should have waited to have those kids. She wasn't ready, and neither was that no-good Jason."

Jess had always considered Marisol—five years her senior—the beauty of their family. In fact, she was the reason Jess had gotten involved in pageants to begin with—she'd wanted to be just like her big sister when she grew up. Back then Marisol had had it all … or so Jess had thought. But when she was twenty, she'd gotten knocked up by Jason, her on-again-off-again boyfriend. Their "off again" periods usually followed her catching him cheating, but for some inexplicable reason, Marisol always took him back. When she'd become pregnant with Jason Junior, she'd dropped out of college, and she and Jay got married. Two years later and pregnant with their second kid, she found out he'd been cheating on her *again*. The ink wasn't even dry on their divorce papers when their second son was born. Marisol was a good mother, but it hadn't always been easy on her. Jess knew that. They *all* knew it. That's why she, Robert, and Manny took the opportunity to help out whenever they could. That was just how their family worked. They'd grown up with a single mother themselves, and they all knew how hard it was. But while Marisol had grown closer to their brothers as her sons had grown up, she and Jess had somehow drifted further apart.

Never once in all these years had Jess considered her sister could be envious of her; she'd just assumed she'd done something to anger Marisol but couldn't figure out what it might have been. Now, hearing her abuela's theory, Jess wondered if the older woman wasn't on to something.

"I don't know, maybe." She shrugged and nibbled on a chip. She loved her grandma's guacamole, but the fats from the avocado did better things for her hair than they did for her thighs. She'd be better off going home and applying it as a conditioning mask than she would by filling her belly with it.

"There's no maybe about it," her grandmother declared as she headed back to the stove. "Now go tell your sister and those boys to help your papa bring in the meat, and we can finally eat. I'm starving."

Jess rose and planted a kiss on her grandmother's cheek. "You're the best."

The other woman pretended to wave away the praise but then smiled. "I really am."

* * *

Jess stepped outside, the warm evening breeze a welcome respite from the fragrance of her grandmother's cooking. A woman on a life-long diet could only be surrounded by the delicious smell of onions, garlic, and tomatoes for so long without pushing everyone to the side and shoving her head inside the pot.

At least out here, she could stand down-wind from the grill. And honestly, except for her grandmother's meatballs, Jess wasn't really a beef girl anyway. Just another way she differed from everyone else in her family. While her brothers could put away literal pounds of carne asada and her sister had never met a tri-tip she didn't like, Jess stuck to the grilled zucchini her papa always made especially for her instead.

"Hey, you guys," Jess said as she came up alongside her siblings. "Soup's almost ready, so Abuela wants everyone to head inside."

Manny finished typing something on his phone, and then shoved the device into his back pocket. "That was Rosalie. She needs me to pick up Abigail."

"I thought it was her weekend," Marisol sneered, hefting one of the platters and turning toward the house. There was no love lost between Marisol and Rosie, whose younger sister was one of the girls Jason had cheated on Marisol with. Marisol couldn't believe her brother would betray her by literally sleeping with the enemy, while *he* failed to understand how Rosalie was responsible for her sister's behavior. It was an argument Jess could practically recite by heart.

"It is, but something came up."

Robert rolled his eyes. "That seems to happen a lot lately." He wasn't a fan of Rosalie either, but that stemmed more from the fact that when she had come into the picture, Manny hadn't been able to act as his wingman anymore. At thirty-five, Robert Casillas-Moore was the biggest ladies' man Jess knew.

"It is what it is." Manny sighed and grabbed the other platter, while Jess picked up the small plate of vegetables and raced to catch up with her siblings.

"It doesn't have to be," Robert said, as Jess fell into step next to them.

"He's right. You should talk with your lawyer again about the custody arrangement." She knew her advice wasn't wanted, but she couldn't help it.

Manny shot her an angry look as Robert jogged ahead to hold the door open for them. "And do what—ask for full-time custody? You know I can't do that."

"Why?" Jess honestly didn't get it. Manny was a talented animator who worked from home, so he had plenty of time for his daughter. And his house, while small like Jess's, was a much better environment than his ex-wife's place in what real estate agents liked to call a "transitional neighborhood." The real issue, she suspected, was that Manny's new girlfriend Camila didn't want his young daughter around. Camila was smart and beautiful, but she also had a jealous streak a mile wide and a foot deep. The fact that Jess's brother had been married before did *not* sit well with her.

Frankly, Jess didn't see their relationship working out in the long run, but what did she know about things like that? She hadn't been on a real date in six months and hadn't had a boyfriend in way longer than that.

Which her brother, of course, was always quick to point out. He pushed his way through the door with a huff. "Honestly, Jess. You are so naive sometimes."

"Manuel Joseph Casillas Moore! You be nice to your sister." With a look that brooked no argument, their grandma set a big, steaming bowl of soup in the middle of the table.

Manny's jaw ticked, and Jess knew he was biting back a smart-ass reply. He shook his head and joined Marisol on the opposite side of the room. Setting his platter down next to hers on the antique oak sideboard, he turned and crossed his arms over his chest. "Someday you're going to have to grow up and join the rest of us adults in the real world. Maybe then you'll understand."

Marisol snorted and rolled her eyes. "Not likely. Jess is waiting for Prince Charming to come along and sweep her off her feet. Everything will be perfectly sickening, and they'll spend all their time riding around on unicorns and living in their made-up fairytale world."

Jess felt tears springing into her eyes. Her sister's idea of humor felt a lot more like an attack. She breathed deeply and stared hard at her siblings, wondering when they'd become so bitter. Wondering what she'd ever done to deserve this treatment. All three stared back, the look on each of their faces defiant and stubborn.

She looked away first. She didn't have the energy for this today. "I'm sorry, abuela, but I'm not hungry anymore. If you'll excuse me—" She darted across the room and grabbed her purse, rushing out the front door before anybody could stop her. She cried for the entire fifteen-minute journey back to her house.

When she pulled into the driveway, her stomach rumbled loudly. Of course.

Jess slammed her palm against the steering wheel. She let out a frustrated growl and pushed herself out of the car.

Stalking angrily up the walk, she unlocked her front door and stepped over the threshold, tossing her purse on the table to her right. At least now she wouldn't have to work off her grandmother's meal by adding an extra mile to tomorrow's run.

Unbidden, her thoughts flashed to the man standing outside The Breadery. The one with dark, haunted eyes and overgrown scruff. The one who'd set her heart racing even more than it already had been. The one who'd stared at her and who she'd stared right back at. Briefly, Jess wondered what had made his eyes so sad, and if he'd seen her own sadness reflected back at him.

Hmm. Maybe she'd keep that extra mile after all.

CHAPTER 3

"Come over for dinner on Friday." Noah's voice was firm through Sean's phone. "Angelica's trying some new recipe Max taught her."

"You have a backup plan?"

Angelica's cooking lessons with Max had been going on for nearly a year, and the results were still pretty hit or miss. Having been subject to a few of the misses, Sean was more than a little dubious. Not to mention, he wasn't sure he felt like having his friends checking up on him. He hadn't had a drink in the two weeks since they'd pulled their dirty little trick. He hadn't bothered to test their homegrown prohibition movement by ordering one in River Hill. Max's word was gold around town, and Angelica's was, too. He'd thought about heading out of town to get one, but the effort hadn't seemed worth it—nor the cost of the Uber back home afterward.

Plus, he'd been secretly enjoying his mornings recently. Now that he was sober enough to notice, he'd seen the same gorgeous jogger several times over the last week. Every day, she'd slowed down as she passed the bakery and sniffed the air, the pure enjoyment coming over her face making his groin tighten. They'd exchanged smiles, and she'd jogged on. It was quickly becoming a morning tradition he looked forward to.

Not that he had much else to look forward to. "I'll come for dinner," he said.

"Good. I was beginning to wonder if you'd hung up on me." The concern in Noah's voice was real, even though he was obviously trying to keep it light.

"I'll save that for after dinner."

"If it's that bad, we'll order pizza."

"You promise?"

"I solemnly swear," Noah said. "Just don't tell Angelica."

"Tell me what?" The faint voice in the background was Noah's girlfriend. Sean heard a door closing.

"Um." Noah's voice faded, and Sean decided he must have put his hand over the phone to tell her some blatant lie.

"I'm hanging up for real now," he said. "Good luck with that."

"See you Friday," Noah said. "Bring dessert."

Sean rolled his eyes even though his friend wasn't there to see it. "You got it." He always brought dessert. It was the obvious choice, but suddenly it seemed so dull. He hung up the phone with a sigh. At least when he was drinking, he didn't notice how empty his life was.

He knew he ought to be grateful for his friends' intervention. He'd realized recently that without drinking, his evenings were suddenly completely free. He didn't have any hobbies; since he'd come home to River Hill, all he'd done was work and drink. It was a depressing realization. He'd been *fun* in L.A.

Of course, that had been the problem. Possibly. Maybe. He still wasn't sure how much of what had happened was his fault. Had he set the party-boy example that had led Cal to emulate him? He'd never been a drug user himself, but he'd been to plenty of parties where they'd been there for the taking, and he'd been cheerfully vocal about his exciting lifestyle when he'd convinced the kid to sign with the record label he'd worked for. Had tempted him with modern day visions of sugarplums: girls, booze, and money. It was the standard line. Cal Grissom had been a kid from Kentucky with a raw talent that had landed him millions of internet followers for his homemade videos. Sean had found him, signed him, and produced his debut album. It had gone platinum immediately, and everything Sean had promised him had come true.

And then something had gone wildly wrong. Cal had gone dark on him, stopped answering his phone. When he didn't show up for a promotional spot, Sean had gone looking for him. He had a key to the hotel room—another standard policy, in case artists got out of line and emergency cleanup or a PR push was needed. He'd let himself in, calling the kid's name. At first, he'd thought Cal was sleeping, and he'd let himself get annoyed. He'd said a few things out loud about irresponsible, ungrateful teenagers. It was only when he'd gotten closer to the bed that he'd realized that Cal wasn't listening. Wouldn't ever listen again. Or sing … or look up at him with that goofy grin that said he'd just thought of a new line for a song. Cal was dead, and it was Sean's fault.

The inquiry had cleared him of any official blame. The police hadn't ever really considered him a suspect—they'd only questioned him because he was the first to discover the body. It was so obviously an overdose that the officer on the scene had merely nodded and said, "Tough break. My kids love him."

It happened every day in L.A., but Sean hadn't been able to shake the feeling that it was his fault. He was the one who'd sold Cal on how great all the extra perks of being the world's biggest pop star were. Cal had listened to him with wide eyes the first few weeks. Then, at some point, he'd leaped in, spending most of his free nights at ridiculous parties dancing with coked-out actresses and their junkie friends. And Sean hadn't stopped him. Truth be told, he hadn't even noticed, until he'd been forced to. And now he couldn't escape the guilt—even here in River Hill, which might as well be light years away from L.A. Especially not sober.

"Damn kid." Sean scrubbed his palm across his face, stubble scraping the skin. He needed to shave before he went to sleep tonight. No time to do it in the mornings, not when he had to be at the bakery so early. He generally rolled out of bed and into his clothes and out the door.

It was another far cry from his L.A. days. But a complete break was what he'd needed. The label had accepted his resignation with a shrug; he was a good producer, but he was one of many. At home, he was a little more than that. He was the only son, the darling of the Amorys. He was a baker. He'd learned how to shape dough at the same time as he'd learned to read; he'd cracked eggs and measured flour as soon as he could toddle to the counters. Baking had been in his life forever. His parents had been disappointed when he'd insisted on taking a different career path. When his father had died ten years ago, he'd given serious thought to coming back, but he'd just signed his first big client, and his mom had shaken her head. "You're doing what you want to do," she'd said quietly. "I'll manage."

He'd assumed she would call one of the distant Amory cousins and ask if they wanted to start learning about the business. There was no way The Breadery would ever leave the Amory family. But she'd just hired a few extra hands, and life in River Hill had continued on as usual.

And then he'd come home, and she hadn't said a word, just nodded when he'd asked for the morning shift and adjusted the schedules. She'd opened up the apartment that his grandfather had built over the garage for one of the cousins a long time ago and bought him some new curtains for it. She'd handed him the key and invited him for dinner while he got set up, and then they'd just…. moved on. She lived her life, he lived his, intersecting occasionally at the bakery or the house. She'd never asked him anything about Cal. He was sure she'd read the articles; she'd known Cal was his client. He'd sent her a few of the videos when he'd signed the kid. And Cal's death had been all over the news until some celebrity had been caught cheating on his wife with a housekeeper.

Now, as he shaved, he reflected that his mother was biding her time to see what he was going to do. That was the sort of person she was. She'd never been the sort of mom who interfered in his life, but she'd always somehow known what he was going to do before he did it. He had no idea if she was aware of how bad his drinking had gotten, but Angelica's threat of telling her had undoubtedly worked on him. His mother didn't deserve to be dragged through the mud with him. He'd begged the record label to put pressure on the media not to talk about his hometown or his family during the inquiry, something they'd agreed to do as one last favor.

He sighed. Noah's call had come while he was doing his usual—nothing. He'd gone through a few emails from old colleagues and friends and surfed the internet aimlessly for a while. He'd checked on a few market trends—cake balls were still a hot topic, but his mother refused to allow them in The Breadery. Secretly, he agreed with her. Nobody should treat cake that way.

He wiped down the sink and headed back to the

bedroom. The apartment was nice enough—far more spacious than the studio space over Max's garage that Iain had once occupied. But it was still a far cry from his place in L.A. He stripped down to his boxers and flipped the covers back on the bed, reflecting once again that if he was committing to staying in River Hill, he really ought to get his own place. One that had room for a bigger bed than a full-sized mattress.

But he still had no idea if he was going to stay. It had been two years, and the idea of going back to L.A. still made him nauseous and shaky. But the thought of staying here, in sleepy River Hill, where it seemed like the only thing he knew to do was drink or stay home, didn't entirely appeal either. So he stayed here, at his mother's house, in a strange sort of limbo.

He slid into the bed and let himself imagine coming up against another body there, maybe the girl he kept seeing jogging past the bakery. Warm skin, long hair, full lips, perfect breasts… He reached down and took himself in hand. If he wasn't going to have company in bed, he could at least pretend. Lord knew he'd been doing plenty of that lately.

* * *

THE NEXT MORNING, Sean let his hands move through the motions of opening the bakery without paying much attention, still occupied by the questions that had been nagging at him all night. His sleep had been fitful—not great for the early shift. He mixed, poured, kneaded, and shaped dough mechanically, flicking muffin tins and sheet trays in and out of the enormous ovens. It was Tuesday, so he made his specialty—apple fritters. They were Naomi's favorite too —she and Iain would almost certainly be in to pick up a few later in the morning.

He paused in the middle of chopping apples, the knife coming to rest on the board with a *thunk* as he remembered with an internal wince that he was only in the habit of making fritters on Tuesdays because that was when he'd been sober enough to handle a sharp knife safely. The Hut closed early on Monday nights. He smirked and tossed a piece of apple into his mouth. Maybe he'd surprise Naomi with a fritter delivery on Thursday, just to watch her face. It was hard to surprise the cool and collected Miss Klein, though Iain had made her a little less buttoned up these days.

He finished chopping the fruit and added it to the bowl with the dough, then dug in with his hands to create the lumpy balls that would go into the fryer before being covered in a light glaze. His thoughts wandered back to Naomi, then on to Iain, her boyfriend, although she still winced at the term. Iain sold whiskey for a living. His family was practically royalty in Ireland, as they'd been in the distilling business of for generations. Iain and his sister had brought a new blend to California last year, and their sales were going gangbusters. Sean looked down at the fritters he'd been shaping. "Whiskey glaze," he murmured aloud. "Wonder if Mom would go for it."

Probably not. The Breadery didn't embrace new things. Even the fritter recipe had come from one of his grandfather's books. Or maybe his great-grandfather. The front room of his mother's house was lined with shelves that held the Amory Recipes, sacred hand-written books from generations of bakers. Her pet project was digitizing them. He'd bought her a top of the line scanner a few years ago, and she'd been working to scan page after page of crabby Amory handwriting ever since.

He dumped the empty bowl in the sink and carried the apple peels and cores to the compost bin by the back exit.

He glanced at his watch. *Trash time.* If he were lucky, he'd catch his fantasy girl again. He pulled the bag and spun it closed as he opened the door. There she was, just rounding the corner. Today she was wearing teal compression leggings with mesh panels along the thighs, and his mouth watered at the glimpse of skin they revealed. He tossed the bag into the dumpster as she began her usual slow-down-and-sniff routine.

Normally, he just leaned against the wall and exchanged a smile with her. Today, thoughts of his future in River Hill whirling in his head, he stepped forward. "Hi."

She came to a stop and met his eyes. "Hi."

"Um, I'm Sean." He wasn't entirely sure what to do, now that he'd initiated this conversation. He reached out a hand.

She set her hand in his, and they shook. Her grasp was warm and firm, the skin of her hands soft. "I'm Jess."

"Nice to meet you."

"You too. You work here?"

"Yeah." He didn't qualify it with specifics. He didn't need to impress her with his last name. At least, not yet.

"You do good work. Smells amazing." She smiled, and it was like the sun rising a second time that morning.

"Thanks."

"I'll see you around, Sean," she said. "Gotta finish my run."

He nodded. "Have a good morning."

"You too." She inhaled one last deep breath, and he couldn't help himself—his eyes dropped to her incredible breasts. He dragged them back up in time to see her grinning at him before she took off again.

He leaned against the wall, running a hand through his hair. *Jess.* At least now he had a name to go with his dreams.

CHAPTER 4

The TV station's makeup artist dabbed at a shiny spot on Jess's nose, while a frazzled assistant called out the countdown to showtime from across the set. "I'm sorry." She continued to forcefully buff and polish Jess's face. "I can't get the color to blend properly."

Jess held in a sigh. This wasn't the first time she'd heard that. Honestly, she didn't get it. She was Mexican-American, but she had a relatively light, smooth complexion. And it wasn't like brown skin was that uncommon in California. Perhaps it was the abundance of freckles dotting the bridge of her nose and cheekbones—courtesy of her father's genetics—that was the problem. *Damn Irish roots.* She'd rather blame the freckles than assume every single makeup artist she'd ever met was vaguely racist.

"That's all right," she said trying not to let her frustration show. "I carry my own foundation, if that'll help."

Over the years, she'd learned what makeup worked on her skin tone and what didn't. Unfortunately, the former was a much shorter list than the latter. Carrying a brand she knew would do the job under any circumstance meant she was often able to head off disaster at the pass. She hoped this would be one of those times, because by the look on the other woman's face, whatever she was using was *not* up to the task.

Her nose scrunched with disapproval. "I'm not supposed to, but ..." She cast her eyes about the cordoned-off space to make sure no one was paying attention. "We're only supposed to use the brands that have been approved. Something about—"

Her words were cut off by a harried-looking assistant carrying a clipboard and an iPad. "Is she done?"

The makeup artist looked between Jess and her co-worker, and Jess saw the moment the woman decided to throw her to the wolves instead of fixing the bad makeup job. "Yeah, she'll do."

"But—" Jess started to say when the assistant grabbed her hand and pulled her out of her chair. The makeup artist mouthed "sorry" as she was dragged away.

Jess tipped her head back and looked to the heavens. *Ay, dios mío,* she thought as the assistant led behind the anchor's desk. Following the commercial break, she was supposed to sit there and speak authoritatively on the season's best beauty trends ... all while looking like a damn fool. Some expert she was.

Sylvia Barrows, the anchor for this hour of programming, stepped around Jess to sit in her raised chair. "You have something on your nose," she said, pointing at her own face and twirling her finger.

Jess sighed. "Yeah, there was some ... difficulty." She felt bad throwing the makeup artist under the bus. It wasn't her fault she didn't know how to blend foundation properly. *Wait, no.* She shook her head and rolled her eyes inwardly. If it wasn't the woman's fault for not knowing how to do her job properly, then whose was it? Certainly not Jess's. "Suffice it to say; brown skin doesn't seem to be her forte."

Sylvia glanced at the countdown clock across the room, and then covertly passed Jess a moist baby wipe. A kind smile stretched her expertly-lined lips. "You don't have enough time to fix it properly, but you can wipe most of it off before the camera rolls. You might wind up shiny, but at least you'll be the right color."

"Thanks." Jess turned in her seat to hide the shoddy work she was surreptitiously undoing.

"No problem," Sylvia said, gesturing to a small waste bin at their feet. "My sister-in-law is Mexican, so I get it."

Before Jess could respond, Sylvia held up her index finger and tapped her ear. Then, she sat up straight in her chair, her demeanor suddenly all business-like.

"Hello, and welcome to your favorite morning news broadcast," she began a few seconds later. "This hour, we'll bring you live reports from the fires raging down in Santa Barbara, as well as news on the proposed teachers' strike in Marin. But first, let's get your morning started on a more positive note. Today we're welcoming Jessica Casillas-Moore back to the show. Jess is here to discuss the season's biggest trends. Good morning, Jess."

Sylvia swiveled in her chair to face Jess, her cue to launch into her prepared remarks. Suddenly, however, she didn't feel like she could say what she'd planned to. The station had brought her in as an expert, and she didn't look the part right now.

Jess knew she had a choice to make. She could either phone it in and hope the audience wasn't too vicious when they tore her to shreds for her appearance (which would result in the station never inviting her back, as well as a storm of negative comments on her own blog), or she could get real with the audience and hope she wasn't blacklisted.

Either way, she probably wouldn't get another opportunity to show her face in studio 3B again after this morning. She firmed her jaw. If she was going to be ripped to shreds by assholes in the comments section online regardless of which path she chose, it might as well be because she'd delivered some hard, honest truths.

"Good morning, Sylvia, and thank you for inviting me back." Jess flashed the smile that had won her a dozen or more trophies, and then slumped over theatrically and ran her fingers through her hair. Or at least tried to. While the makeup person the station used might not have known her craft, their hairstylist was no joke. Jess's hair was *not* moving.

With a self-deprecating laugh, she dropped her hands onto the counter. "Honestly, I'd love to tell you all about the best corduroy jeggings to fit your body type, or why nude lipstick is all the rage, but as you can see from my face, today is *not* going the way I'd intended. So instead, I wanted to talk to you about something else." She gestured toward her freckled nose, on full view to the camera.

Jess let her eyes slide to Sylvia to see if she was going to put a stop to the change of topic, but the other woman smiled and said, "I think all of us can say we've been there. What mom hasn't?"

Jess wasn't a mom, but sure, she'd play right along—especially since she knew most of the program's viewers were parents. "As you can tell from my name, I'm a bit of a mutt—a mixture of Mexican on my mom's side, and Irish-American on my dad's. That means sometimes all this—" she raised her hand and rotated her finger in front of her face "—can pose a bit of a challenge in the makeup department. And I know I'm not alone. As Sylvia said, we've all been there." She took a deep breath and plunged on.

"And while there are days where we might want to say to heck with it, the reality is, we can't. How many times have you skipped your blush, only for your co-worker Greg to mention that you look a bit tired today? Or, when you didn't fill in your brows, the guy at the coffee shop remarked that it looked like you could really use that double espresso? Or, how about when you pick up your kid at school, another mom asks if you're getting enough sleep." She leaned toward the camera, hoping it would pick up her earnesty.

"Every day, we put on our faces … not necessarily because we want to, but because we *have* to. Otherwise, we'd spend all our waking hours justifying the looks we were born with. Take me, for example. I guarantee you, twenty minutes after this program airs, the station's Twitter feed will be flooded with 'helpful' comments about the ugly woman who was there to deliver beauty advice." She raised her hands and used her fingers to make air quotes.

"You ain't kidding," Sylvia whispered under her breath.

Jess cast her a quick, conspiratorial grin. As one of the area's leading news anchors, Jess knew how much time Sylvia spent in hair and makeup. No way was the local news putting a woman on air who didn't look perfectly coiffed and painted.

Jess sat up straight and took a deep breath. Through the glare of the studio lights, she couldn't see what the reaction to her sidebar was, but no one had rushed the stage or cut her mic, so she figured they were going to let her finish the segment. "Now, since the station invited me here to give you some beauty advice, with my remaining few minutes, I want to offer you a handful of quick tips on how to spend as little time possible looking your best."

"First, get at least eight hours of sleep." She rolled her eyes deliberately as if to say, 'yeah, I know, that's garbage advice.'

"I know, I know." She shook her head. "Who has time for that, right? Since no woman I'm familiar with does, here's my second recommendation: drink as much water as possible.

It'll flush the toxins out of your body and help hydrate your skin from the inside.

"Third, always use moisturizer. Don't worry. I'm not talking about that thousand-dollar-a-jar stuff either. Good old Oil of Olay is what all the women in my family use and several of us are pageant winners." She flashed a saucy grin, as though she'd just aced the talent portion.

"Fourth, if you only have time for one item of makeup, *always* make it mascara. It'll make your eyes pop, which will make it look like you actually did get those precious eight hours of sleep, and then the lovely Greg will be forced to keep his trap shut."

Sylvia stifled a laugh next to her, which turned into a very real cough.

Jess set her elbow on the counter and rested her chin in her palm, her fingers brushing against her cheek. Putting on an exasperated tone, she added, "And finally, always carry baby wipes in case you find yourself needing to remove foundation three shades darker than your normal skin tone. No one wants an orange band around their face." She smiled at the audience through the camera, and the light turned red.

"And … go to commercial."

Jess slid out of her chair and unclipped the mic from the neck of her sweater. She didn't know if she'd just committed career suicide or garnered herself a whole slew of new fans. Either way, her segment certainly hadn't been routine. People could say what they wanted to about her, but one thing was certain—Jess Casillas-Moore wasn't boring.

"That was … refreshing," Sylvia commented, standing and adjusting the waistband of her skirt. From the way she shimmied and swung her hips, Jess was pretty sure the woman was wearing two layers of Spanx under the heavy wool of her suit.

Jess smiled and fluffed out her hair, shaking her long

mahogany curls loose from their stiffened prison of style. Goodness, she hated hairspray. "Thanks. I know it wasn't the segment the producers brought me in to deliver, but I couldn't sit there looking like this and risk my professional reputation. No one wants to take beauty advice from a woman who looks like a hot mess."

"Unless she starts by acknowledging it," Sylvia answered.

Jess nodded. "Exactly."

"Well, I'm not sure how my bosses upstairs are going to react, but personally, I thought the segment was a success." She tilted her head to the side and pursed her lips. "In fact, would you be open to doing more like it?"

"Come again?"

"If I can get the producers on board, how would you feel about being a regular guest? Say, a weekly bit where you come on and give straight-talk beauty advice. None of this 'how to look great during bikini season' nonsense—none of us look great in a bikini, and we all know it—but rather real, practical advice for real, practical women." Sylvia's enthusiasm was evident in her tone, getting brighter as she went on.

Wow. That certainly wasn't what Jess had expected when she'd decided to go rogue with her spot. At best, she'd anticipated being told she'd never be welcomed back; at worst, escorted out of the building and tossed into the parking lot like a used rag doll. "That sounds … really great, actually. Provided, of course, your producers are willing to let me back in the building after today."

Over Jess's shoulder, Sylvia scanned the room from left to right. "If the smiling faces around here are any indication, I think it's a genuine possibility."

Jess turned to take in the mood of the people around her. True to Sylvia's word, no one looked angry. She wouldn't go so far as to say they seemed happy, but they weren't *unhappy* either. Perhaps she hadn't screwed up her career after all.

When Jess turned back around, Sylvia passed her a business card. "Here's my contact information. Touch base with me in a week or so, and I'll let you know how our weekly programming discussion went." She leaned in close. "It's not widely publicized, but my contract stipulates I have power of refusal over interviews. I've only invoked it once—a tech CEO accused of sexual harassment. It's about time the producers and I discussed the people I *want* to welcome to the stage during my hour of programming." She tossed Jess a conspiratorial grin.

Jess pulled out her wallet out of her purse and tucked the card into it before shrugging the leather satchel back up onto her shoulder. "Ms. Barrow, if any woman in the Bay Area has earned the right to interview who she wants, it's you. You're a local institution."

Sylvia smiled beatifically. "Please, feel free to tell my bosses."

"You get me this gig, and I'll tell them anything you want."

Sylvia extended her hand, and Jess clasped it. "You keep delivering fresh commentary like what you just did, and I just might let you."

Ten minutes later, Jess signed herself out of the studio and made her way to her trusty Honda Accord. Her morning certainly hadn't gone the way she'd thought it would when she'd driven here during the pre-dawn hours, but that just proved you never knew what the day might hold.

Unbidden, her mind flashed to the handsome man outside The Breadery. She hadn't expected *him* either, but he was another recent, happy surprise. They'd barely spoken a few words—theirs was more of a wave and a smile type of acquaintance—but now she wondered why that was. She was intrigued, and she thought the same held true for him.

She'd taken a huge chance today with that off-the-cuff segment. It had been terrifying, but in the end, ultimately rewarding. Was this the new Jess? Could she work up the courage to go off-script with the baker too? Could he be another reward? There was only one way to find out.

CHAPTER 5

*S*ean reached behind his back to untie the strings of his apron with a practiced flick of his fingers. He eased the neckband of the white canvas over his head and crumpled the flour-covered fabric around the embroidered logo that had been resting across his chest while he worked. He tossed it into the hamper waiting near the door and adjusted the white tee he'd worn underneath, shaking out any remaining crumbs. End-of-shift ritual complete, he poked his head back into the front of the shop and gave a nod to his replacement and a casual wave to the two customers in line to pay for pastries.

"See you later, Mr. Hughes," he called to the one he recognized as one of Naomi and Iain's friendly neighbors.

"Thanks for making extra almond croissants, Sean," Paolo Morrison said as he handed one of them off to the customer Sean didn't recognize. "Don't know how you knew we'd need them."

Sean shrugged. "It's a gift."

"Psychic baker, huh?" Paolo chuckled. "River Hill really does have it all." Paolo was a student at the community college on the other side of town. His parents had moved here last year, and Paolo had worked at The Breadery during his senior year of high school, bumping up his hours once his college schedule became more flexible. He was a good kid. Sean tried to ignore the flash of nausea thinking about Paolo's bright future gave him. Best not to let the kid get too close, or he might ruin it the way he'd destroyed Cal's.

"See you tomorrow, Paolo," he said, getting a nod in return as the younger man concentrated on the register.

Sean slipped out the back door, taking one last load of trash with him to toss into the dumpster on the way to his truck. He smiled fondly at his beloved steed as he approached. The vintage blue behemoth wasn't to everyone's taste, but Sean adored it. It had been his grandfather's, and he'd found it sitting untouched in the storage garage behind his mother's house when he'd moved home, the turquoise paint job perfectly intact underneath decades of dust. His mother had laughed when he'd asked about it.

"It's been sitting there for God knows how long," she'd said. "I'd almost forgotten about it."

"You and Dad never drove it?"

"Your father was a sedan sort of man," she said with a grin. "And I never learned to drive a stick, to be honest."

He'd cheerfully offered her his Audi on the spot. And now he was the proud owner of Bessie Blue, the cutest truck in River Hill. She'd served him well over the last couple of years. And he'd collected a *lot* of notches in his bedpost from the women who were charmed when he showed up to deliver the Breadery's cupcakes to parties in Bessie Blue. He grinned as he fired up the engine. He'd needed a few tune-ups along the way, but she still ran like a dream.

He drove the three miles to his mother's house in the same vague state of appreciation and annoyance he'd been in for months. River Hill was still the same beautiful, charming town he'd grown up in. He drove past houses he'd played in as a kid, most fronted by picket fences or with roses climbing over trellises. On drives like this, it felt like nothing ever changed here. It was one of the reasons he'd left, long ago. But things *were* different. A new crop of businesses surrounded the Breadery on the town square, a new crowd of people his own age bumped into him in line at the coffee shop. River Hill was revitalizing. And he was different, too. He just wasn't sure what kind of different he was. The kind who could go back to his high-powered life in L.A., albeit with a few safety-conscious changes? Or the type who would settle in the town he'd grown up in, helping it change for the better?

He pulled into the driveway still mulling the question and spied his mother's car parked in front of the garage. Somehow, it reminded him that he'd promised to bring dessert to dinner with Noah and Angelica tomorrow night— and wouldn't Noah be thrilled to hear that Sean was reminded of him when he thought of his mother? He smirked as he headed to the door of his mom's house instead of the private entrance to his apartment out back.

"Mom?"

"In here!" Her voice came from the formal living room she'd converted to a library and office. The door off the foyer was ajar, and Sean stepped in.

Mary Amory was sitting at the antique desk she'd haggled from an estate sale years ago, dark hair in a loose bun and bare feet up on the pitted surface of the desk as she flipped through yet another family recipe book. "How was work?" She closed the book and smiled up at him, the same warm smile that had felt like a benediction when he'd come home a shambles of a man two years prior.

"Made extra almond croissants," he said.

"Did we need them?"

"Seemed like it. Paolo was selling them as I left."

She nodded. "You're getting better."

He laughed. "The famous Amory Gift?" There wasn't one, to the best of his knowledge, but it had been a family joke as long as he could remember.

"I was thinking more like a basic understanding of supply and demand," his mother answered dryly.

"Ouch. I took Econ 301 in college, I'll have you know."

"Yes, and I'm very proud." She dropped her feet down on the floor and leaned forward to replace the book she'd been holding on the stack next to the scanner. "Did you want something? I'm going to scan a few more pages and then I'm heading out."

"Got a hot date?" He was teasing, but he was startled to see his mother's cheeks color slightly.

"Maybe."

"Mom, are you getting back on the horse?" This was a far more interesting topic than the one he'd come here for. He swung the dining chair that sat opposite the desk around and straddled it, leaning his arms on its back and his chin on his fist. "Tell me eeeeeeverything."

"I will tell you nothing, you gossip."

"*Me?*"

"Yes, you. I know perfectly well how word spreads in this town. I've lived here my entire life." His mother had grown up in this very house. Mary Amory had taken her future as the owner of The Breadery so seriously she'd never changed her name when she'd married his father, and somehow, they'd agreed to give their only child the family name, too. She'd always laughed and said the situation wasn't so unusual because they'd gotten married in the seventies.

"Keep your secrets, then," he said with a chuckle. "But I'm glad to see you're having fun."

"I am," she said with a smile. "Ten years is a long time."

"It sure is. What made you finally open up?" He winced. "Let's pretend I didn't use those words because I really don't want to think about my mother that way."

"Pot, kettle," she said. "Think I don't know how many women have been in that apartment over the last two years?"

"Hey, you made this," he said, gesturing toward his body dramatically. "Shouldn't you be proud that people appreciate it?"

She rolled her eyes. "I'd rather you appreciate yourself."

"Gross, mom."

"Sean Amory, you know that wasn't what I meant."

He laughed. "You set yourself up for it."

"You're so charming; I can't imagine why even *more* women aren't throwing themselves at your feet."

His mind flashed suddenly to the pretty jogger he'd introduced himself to. Jess, she'd said her name was. "Me neither," he answered, his thoughts focused on the pretty brunette.

"Anyway, I need to go get ready."

"Before you do, can I borrow a few recipe books?"

She paused in the middle of standing up, her hands braced on the desk. "The books?"

He nodded. "I'm supposed to make a dessert to take to Noah and Angelica's for dinner tomorrow, and I thought I might surprise them with something different."

His mother looked at him, her dark eyes thoughtful. "Different?"

He shrugged, uncomfortable under her scrutiny. "Sure. Shake things up a little bit."

"I see."

"Actually, I was sort of thinking that we could think about doing the same with The Breadery." *In for a penny, in for a pound.* Might as well see what she thought about his ideas.

"What do you mean?" Her face had gone completely expressionless. Never a good sign.

"There's a lot of new growth in River Hill. I thought maybe we could try a few new things, new recipes to sell."

Her lips thinned. "Probably not."

"Why not?" He frowned. "There are so many great things out there to try."

"We aren't hurting for business, Sean."

"I know, but—"

"I've always stayed true to the way your grandfather and his father and grandfather ran the business," she said firmly. "River Hill loves us the way we are. And if we were to take up oven space making bulk batches of some random new thing we don't even know would sell, it would take bake time and space away from our tried-and-true sellers. We don't have room to add any more ovens, and we aren't in a position to expand, honey. I'm sorry."

He sighed. This wasn't an argument he was prepared to go in-depth on today. He didn't even know if he planned to stay here permanently. Why shake things up with the business if he wasn't going to be around for the fallout? "I get it, Mom. But can I at least steal a corner of the oven for a single batch of something to take to dinner tomorrow after the morning rush?"

"Sure, honey. What about the apple fritters? Your friends love those."

"I'll think about it. But I'm still going to look through a few of these." He gestured toward the shelves surrounding them, lined with books.

"Sounds good." She raised to her full height and gave him that familiar smile. "See you later."

"Have fun on your date, Mom."

"Oh, I will."

"Don't do anything I wouldn't do."

"I think I can limit myself a little more than that," she laughed as she left the room.

* * *

TWO HOURS LATER, Sean tucked the book he'd been flipping through into his nightstand with a sigh. Nothing in the Amory family toolbox of recipes was appealing to his sudden need for something different. Should he look elsewhere for inspiration? He picked up his phone, then put it back down with a shudder. If he weren't careful, he'd wind up trolling Pinterest. He might be feeling a little out of sorts, but he wasn't *desperate.*

He swung his legs over the edge of his bed and stood. He just needed to get out. There was always a chance that inspiration would strike at the market. And if it didn't, he could at least pick up some plums and make a frangipane tart. He tugged a button-down denim shirt over his white tee and headed out towards Bessie Blue and the small grocery store his mother frequented.

At two in the afternoon, the parking lot was relatively empty. One of the virtues of working the morning shift was that he had the afternoons free to roam. Not that he'd taken advantage of it much until recently—until his friends put a stop to it, he'd mostly roamed directly to a bar and parked there until he stopped thinking about his old life back in Southern California. Now he was trying to think about other things.

He made his way inside the store and plucked several slightly under-ripe plums into his basket; he liked them juicier, but for baking, they were better when they were firm. Backup plan firmly in place, he turned slowly in a circle, seeking inspiration. Nothing leaped out at him from the produce section. He sighed and headed toward the spice aisle.

Cinnamon, cloves, ginger, nutmeg ... He traced the familiar names with a finger along the rack of price tags under each little bottle. Each was perfectly common, but not typically used at the bakery. The Amory family had strong French roots, and French pastry was at the heart of all of the recipes Sean knew. He leaned in and picked up a bottle of Ceylon cinnamon, the most expensive one on the shelf, turning it over in his hand thoughtfully. Cinnamon rolls weren't outside the bakery's repertoire, but Sean knew there was so much more that could be done with the deceptively complex spice. If only his mother would give him a shot to prove it.

"It's Sean, right?"

He straightened and turned to see who was asking, and felt a slow smile spread as he came face-to-face with the dark-haired jogger he'd been dreaming about smiling back at him.

"Hi. Yeah, it's Sean. You're Jess, right?" Maybe something different had been right here all along.

CHAPTER 6

*J*ess's heart was racing. In the middle of the grocery store. And she wasn't even standing in the cereal aisle. All in all, her reaction to the sexy baker standing next to her was very out of the ordinary.

Get it together, woman.

She pushed her shoulders back and took a deep breath. With a shaky grin, she canted her head toward the little glass jar that was dwarfed by Sean's surprisingly elegant hand. It didn't look like it belonged to someone who worked around hot ovens all morning long. In fact, his cuticles were as manicured as hers were. "Picking up spices for the bakery?"

"Pardon?" His brows were turned down in confusion.

"The cinnamon?" Jess felt her cheeks heat as she looked at him expectantly.

For several seconds he continued staring at her as if she'd sprouted two heads. Eventually, his gaze followed hers, and then his eyes darted back up. "Oh! No, we order everything in bulk. This is for something different."

"Oh?" She paused, waiting for him to continue. When he didn't, Jess began to wonder if Sean Amory had a screw or two loose in that beautiful dark blonde head of his. Either that, or he had terrible interpersonal skills. Maybe that was why he'd chosen a career where he was done working for the day by the time most other people woke up. "Okay, well, it was nice talking to—"

Sean reached out, his hand hovering tentatively over her shoulder. "Don't go. I'm sorry." He shook his head and blinked, his eyes focusing in on her. "What were you saying?"

"Neither of us were saying much of anything, actually." She smiled at him, acknowledging how awkward their interaction had been so far. "You mentioned you were thinking about making something different. I indicated I'd be interested in hearing more."

He dropped his hand to the side and let out a long sigh. "Honestly, I don't even know what I want to make. I'm going to dinner at my friend's house tomorrow night, and I'm supposed to bring dessert. I didn't want to bring anything from the bakery, though. I was hoping I'd get some inspiration here." He gestured wide as if to encompass the entire store.

They were standing in the middle of aisle six at the local supermercado, located on the outskirts of town. It wasn't unheard of to see white people shopping there, but Jess had been going there her whole life, and she'd never once seen Sean step foot inside. She would have remembered him. A girl didn't forget those chiseled cheekbones and piercing hazel eyes.

She peered into his cart. "Eggs are a good start."

He nodded and rolled his lips between his teeth. "And then I drew a blank."

That was … odd. The man made pastry for a living, and he couldn't come up with inspiration for dessert? Jess didn't often indulge, but when she did, she could attest to the fact that The Breadery made some of the most sinfully decadent confections around. Perhaps Sean's job was to bake the bread, not the sweets.

"Well, what do you like?"

"I like just about everything," he answered. "And so do my friends. But I thought I'd bring something different. Something they wouldn't expect."

Something different. It was hard to pretend Jess didn't wish he'd been talking about her, not food. Or maybe both. Something about this guy just did it for her.

Tamping down those thoughts, she examined the rack of spices. Eventually, her eyes latched onto the ancho chili powder. "How do you feel about something spicy?"

"I can't say I feel one way or the other about it."

"Let me be more specific. Do you like molé?"

"I fucking love molé." He winced. "Sorry. Yes, I love molé."

Jess batted away the apology. "Don't even worry about it. For something as good as my abuela's recipe, any other response would be sacrilege."

Sean smiled at her, the first time since they'd started speaking, and Jess felt it all the way to the tips of her toes. The few times she'd seen him, he'd looked haggard. Like someone who'd been ridden hard and put away wet. Her impression was of a deeply unhappy man. So seeing him smile made her feel like she'd accomplished something worthwhile with her day.

"Good to know," he answered, "but I'm on dessert duty." He cocked his head to the side, raising his eyebrows as though he were daring her to challenge him.

Far be it from her to turn down a dare. Jess grabbed a few different bottles of spices and tossed them into his cart. "Do you think you can trust me?"

He eyed her for a few brief seconds and then shrugged. "As much as I trust anyone, I suppose."

Jess didn't know why, but his response made her

inordinately sad. What sort of man had so few people in his life that he could trust? Admittedly, she didn't have a ton of close personal friends—the pageant world hadn't been conducive to fostering deep, meaningful friendships among women. And these days, blogging for a living generally kept her in front of a screen, not out partying. Surely though, he had to have someone in his life who he trusted above all others. Jess might not get along with her family all that well lately, but she knew in her bones that they'd always have her back. Who had Sean's?

She pushed the question to the back of her mind. She didn't know him well enough to pry.

"Come on. I know exactly what you should make."

He chuckled, but fell in step alongside her, the wheels of their carts rumbling over the mottled linoleum. "You have me intrigued."

Jess tossed him a happy smile. Not one of the fake ones she'd practiced for pageants and TV appearances; an honest-to-goodness one that said *prepare to have your mind blown.* "Good." She looked around, taking stock of their position in the store. "This way." She pushed her cart toward the end of the aisle, expecting he'd follow. "We're going to need dried chilies."

"Chilies?" His eyebrows were raised nearly to his hairline, but he was following her. "What sort of dessert do you have in mind, woman?"

The timbre of Sean's voice skated over Jess's nerve endings. Something about the way he said *woman* had her feeling itchy—like her skin was too small for her frame. The reaction was instantaneous … and unexpected. Sure, she found him handsome, but a lot of men were attractive. There was something about *this one*, though, that had her on high alert. Their conversation might have started out awkward and stilted, but now that he'd relaxed, he was charming and comfortable to be with. And he was easy to look at, too. She wouldn't mind spending more time with him, honestly.

Hmm. Again, unexpected. She was having all kinds of new experiences today, wasn't she?

Jess stopped in front of a large display of clear cellophane bags filled with just about every type of dried chili one could ever need. She scanned the inventory, zeroing in on the dried anchos and pasillas. She grabbed a bag of each and tossed them into her cart. Turning to Sean, she asked, "Pepitas or sesame seeds?"

"I honestly have no idea." He shook his head and laughed, a deep rumbling sound that made her stomach pitch and roll with the urge to touch him.

Fighting her attraction to him, Jess turned back to the task at hand. Tapping the pad of her index finger to her lips, she considered her options. As she did, she caught Sean eyeing her with a spark of … *something* … gleaming in his eyes. Immediately, she dropped her hand away from her mouth. She didn't need his sexy looks to be giving her sexy thoughts. Her body was barreling down that road without any help, and it could use some brakes.

"Let's go with pepitas." She turned her cart in the direction the bulk nuts. Over her shoulder, she added, "The sesame version is *ah-may-zing,* but so much harder to make. We're already stretching the limitations of my skills with this one."

Sean caught up. "Thank you, by the way. I still have no idea what it is you think I'm making, but I appreciate the guidance."

Jess laughed. "Oh, you're not making this. I am." Sean stopped walking, and Jess realized her error. "I mean, assuming you want my help. I … umm … I bulldozed right over you, didn't I?"

Sean's eyes twinkled, and when he smiled, a dimple

popped in his right cheek. *Wow*, Jess thought. *He really is a handsome devil, isn't he?* Handsome or not; she'd taken over his dessert, and he hadn't asked her to.

He nodded and scratched the stubble lining his jaw, a tiny smirk pulling at his lips. "You did."

"I'm sorry." She looked away. "This happens when I get excited about something. I guess I'm used to just plowing my way forward."

"It's okay," he said, his smirk forming into a full-fledged smile. "It's cute."

Jess smiled back. "That might be the kindest thing anyone's ever said about my penchant for bossiness."

He opened his mouth to say something, but then closed it. He scratched his cheek. "So how's this going to work?"

She shrugged, the question catching her off guard. "Umm … I hadn't thought that far ahead, to be honest. Not to be presumptuous or anything—" he chuckled "—but if you want, you can come by my place, and I'll teach you how to make my abuela's Mexican chocolate pie." She skated the toe of her sandal over the scuffed floor as she waited for his response. Jess didn't get nervous, but she swore she could feel her heart banging away in her chest.

Sean shoved his hands into the pockets of his jeans and rocked back on his heels. He dropped his gaze away from hers, and visibly retreated into himself. For a split second, Jess worried she'd stepped over some invisible line, but then he smiled and met her eyes again. "That sounds great." He gestured up the aisle. "Lead on."

Twenty minutes later, Sean was loading Jess's bags into the trunk of her car. Even though she'd repeatedly told him he didn't have to, he'd insisted. And far be it from her to stop someone from lifting and hauling heavy bags of groceries for her. Especially if that someone had back muscles that flexed and pulled with each stretch toward her trunk. His shirt hung looser on him than was the current style, and every time he leaned over, it rode up a bit, exposing golden skin dusted with fine, pale hairs that seemed to sparkle in the sun. Not that Jess was staring or anything.

He closed her trunk and turned to her. "Thank you again."

She waved her hand in front of her face. "No problem. I love cooking, even if I don't get to do it much."

"Oh yeah?"

Jess glanced away. How to tell someone that even though you loved food, you didn't eat much of it because the ten pounds you'd immediately gain could ruin your career? And Sean wasn't just some random someone either. He worked at a bakery, for goodness sake. His livelihood was built on making the very things she'd purposefully gone without for years. He'd think she was insane if she told him she hadn't eaten a single slice of bread in almost three years.

She fell back on her old standby. "Cooking for one isn't nearly as fun."

Unfortunately, standing with Sean, a man who was so handsome it made her eyes hurt, that excuse sounded even more pathetic than usual. If he knew that she willingly denied herself some of life's greatest pleasures for the sake of a paycheck, he'd run in the opposite direction. Here she was, a single woman approaching thirty who'd been on a diet for more than fifteen years and hadn't been on a date in a year. Yeah, she was a real prize.

He surprised her by nodding in understanding, his smile dimming. "Yeah. I hear you."

He looked away again—as if lost in thought—and Jess took the opportunity to study his profile. His jaw ticked, and deep lines formed around his eyes. In that moment, he looked even more tired than he had that first morning she'd spied him standing outside the bakery in the pre-dawn light.

But then all at once, his features cleared, and he brought his face back around. "So, what time do you want me?"

Unbidden, Jess pictured her body pressed to him, their hips rolling in unison.

Goodness. Just that word … *want*. She shivered. It'd been a very long time since a man had made her feel the way this one did. Inexplicably, she wanted to know him … and for him to know her. Both emotionally and physically.

But that wasn't what he'd meant.

With a quick shake of her head, Jess pulled some air into her lungs and pasted a smile onto her face. "How does six work?"

"Six works great." He reached into his back pocket and pulled out his phone, passing it her way. "You should probably give me your number. Just in case."

Was Jess imagining things, or was that a look of … hope … in his eyes? She didn't want to read too much into it, especially given the troubling way her mind and body were in cahoots, but she let herself imagine for a brief moment that she *hadn't* misinterpreted the look on his face. That he was as into her as she was into him.

Jess took the phone and typed her digits and name into the contacts app before passing it back.

He glanced down at the screen, his dimple popping again, and tapped the phone a few times. Her own phone buzzed in her purse, and he smiled at her.

Jess went weak in the knees.

"That's me, so you have my number. Text me your address? I'll see you at six."

She nodded as he backed away toward his car. She was in so much trouble.

CHAPTER 7

Sean was nervous. And he hadn't been nervous about a date with a girl since he was fifteen. This wasn't really a date, though. Or was it? He hadn't worried about *that* question either since he was a teenager. But somehow, he felt like a new person tonight. It wasn't as though he'd been celibate since he'd moved back to River Hill—his mother was right about that. But none of the one-night-stands he'd brought home from the bar had ever offered to teach him how to cook.

He found himself smiling as he tucked one side of his henley shirt into his jeans and picked up the market bag full of spices Jess had made him buy. Whatever this was—date or no date—it was something *very* new. And he was pretty sure he was going to like it.

When he pulled Bessie Blue up in front of Jess's charming little cottage, he took a moment to breathe deeply. The house, like its owner, seemed to radiate life. Pale blue shingle siding and navy shutters were accented by a riot of flowers in long boxes along the porch railings, and he caught a glimpse of a windchime glittering with vibrant red and green glass pieces hanging in the corner near a swing that took up the entire left side of the porch. It looked like it got a lot of use. He let himself picture Jess there, hair in a loose ponytail, curves clad in comfortable clothes, a steaming mug of coffee in her hand. The image was so easy to conjure and seemed so real that it nearly took his breath away. He wanted to see her like that, comfortable and at home. His mental image of Jess smiled up at him as she patted the empty bench next to her.

Sean shook his head. Sobriety was making him hallucinate now. He thought he'd gotten beyond the worst of the aftereffects of pickling his liver for the past year, but maybe the headaches and nausea had just been the beginning. He looked down at the bag of spices on the passenger seat of the truck. Should he even be here? Was it fair to subject somebody as lovely as Jess seemed to be to all his baggage?

He didn't have a chance to decide. The door to the house opened, and Jess's head popped out, eyebrows raised. When she met his eyes and smiled, something inside of him relaxed. He didn't take the time to wonder about what made seeing her feel so good, he just grabbed the bag and hopped out of the truck to follow her inside the house.

"Your place is nice," he said as he handed her the spices.

"Thanks." She led him toward the back of the house. "Kitchen's back here."

They entered a room that made Sean blink. "Wow."

"I know, right? It's the whole reason I bought the place." She grinned at him.

The entire back wall of the house was windows. A French door opened onto a small backyard— Sean glimpsed what looked like a wrought-iron table and two chairs on a little patio before he turned his attention back to the bright, airy kitchen. The cabinets were white, but the countertops were made up of what looked like handmade blue and white tile in a mix of geometric patterns, with stylized birds added in to accent the expanse of the island. He looked closer and realized that the knobs on the cabinets were made from the same ceramic. The kitchen was somehow bright and airy while also feeling cozy and warm. It felt like home.

"It's really nice," he said. It felt like an inadequate description.

"Thanks."

He blinked, realizing that in addition to looking good, the kitchen also smelled good. "What do I smell? Did you start without me?" A warm, nutty odor was coming from the oven.

Jess picked up an oven mitt printed with yellow and blue roosters. "I'm toasting the pepitas so we can get started right away. Once you smell them, they're ready." She opened the oven and leaned over to pull out the tray of toasted seeds. Sean let himself watch. Who wouldn't? That ass was magnificent. It took him longer than it should have to drag his eyes back up to what she was doing on the counter. From the look on her face, he knew she'd noticed, but she didn't say anything. The old Sean would have taken that as a sign that everything was golden, and he would have moved in. Sober Sean, newly fledged Actual Human Being, however, had no idea if it was good or bad that she wasn't commenting on him ogling her ass. He winced. He was a mess. *Get back to the baking, Romeo.*

"What's next?" He moved to hold the stone bowl she was pouring the toasted seeds into.

"We grind these up, then make the crust."

"You're using this to grind them?" He held up the pestle that went with the bowl.

"I'm using that to get them started," she corrected. "I need a new blade for my food processor, to be honest. It can't handle whole nuts and seeds anymore."

He laughed. "And here I thought you were just old-fashioned."

She shrugged. "My abuela uses the molcajete for the whole process. I go to the gym if I want arm muscles." She shot him a quick grin. "Here, you have plenty of muscles already; you grind these." She handed him the stone pestle and stepped back.

He obediently stepped to the counter and began to press the tool into the bowl full of seeds. "Is this some kind of test?"

"Not unless you feel like you need testing." She pulled a blue food processor out of a cabinet underneath the counter and clicked its bowl into place. "Got those broken up?"

"Yep." He lifted the bowl and poured the seeds in.

She plugged the appliance in and put the lid on before hitting the pulse button a few times, coarsely grinding the toasted nuts. "Next we add flour and sugar." She pointed to a narrow door on the side of the kitchen opposite the wall of windows. "Pantry's there, can you get it?"

He crossed behind her, feeling the warmth of her body as they met in between the island and the counter. The kitchen might feel big and airy, but in reality, it was pretty small. Perfect for engineering close encounters. Which she surely wasn't. Was she? He really needed to stop overthinking this. He found flour and sugar in labeled plastic containers and brought them to her. She measured in what she needed, then pulsed the processor a few more times.

"There's a stick of butter melted in the microwave," she said, notching her head toward the corner.

He tsked at her. "The microwave?"

"Don't get uppity with me, baker boy," she said with a laugh. "In the real world, we do what we have to."

He laughed. "I get it." At the bakery, they melted butter in large saucepans— but they also used multiple pounds of butter a day. When he'd lived in L.A., he'd never baked, and he hadn't used the microwave in his fancy condo for much beyond reheating leftovers, but he probably would have melted butter in it eventually. Jess's practical attitude was refreshing. He opened the microwave and pulled out the butter, then drizzled it into the food processor bowl at Jess's direction. A few more pulses and they had a crumb crust.

He watched as Jess pulled two pie tins from the cabinet in the island. "Two?"

"I figured you'd want to taste it before you took it to your friend's place," she said.

"And this way, you get the rest?" he teased.

Her expression went blank. "No, I won't be eating it."

"Uh…"

"You can take them both home," she chirped, as though she hadn't just announced she was helping him make two entire pies she didn't have any intention of eating.

"Tell you what, we can put half in your freezer for later," he said.

She shrugged. "Sure."

She didn't give him time to ask any questions about her pie-eating habits. They pressed the crumb mixture into the pie tins and put them in the oven to bake and set. Then he was hustling around the kitchen gathering more ingredients while she washed the food processor bowl.

He pulled the bags of dried peppers she'd made him buy out of the market bag, together with little bottles of cinnamon and coriander seeds. "What are we doing with all this stuff?"

"Pie filling," she said. "It's like mole, but also pie. You're going to love it."

She was right. The pie filling was like a ganache – something he could make with his eyes closed. But her version involved grinding the peppers and spices up in the stone molcajete— she confessed she'd broken her spice grinder and he resolved to buy her a new one immediately, shaking out his aching arm— before adding them to the cream as it warmed on the stovetop. He held the bowl steady while she poured the hot spiced cream over the chocolate he'd broken up, and the steam rising from the mixture made him want to plunge his face directly in.

After the chocolate had melted, they added eggs to the mixture and poured it into the warm crusts, returning the pies to the oven to bake just long enough for the filling to set.

Jess moved to the sink, and he shook his head. "Nope. There's no way you're washing all these dishes." He put his hands on either side of her waist, intending to move her aside so he could take over, but she turned in his grasp, her mouth opening as if to protest. And then they were facing each other, bodies pinned together by the space between the countertops, her breasts pressing against his chest and her eyes dropping to his lips … and how could he do anything *but* kiss her?

She tasted like cream and sunshine, and the chocolate he'd seen her sneak before they'd melted the rest. His hand slid up her back and to her hair, steadying her as his tongue slipped past her lips, discovering even more sweetness. Her arms came around his neck, and he heard her hum in pleasure as her breath mingled with his.

He wanted to plunge into her warmth, bathe in her sweetness. Instead, he pulled back. As their lips separated, he heard her take a quick breath, and he winced. "I'm sorry. I should have asked."

She was silent for a moment, and he could feel her breath moving against his chin. "You probably should have," she said finally. "I would have said yes, though."

"Thank God."

She laughed and pushed on his chest to free herself. "I think you said something about washing these dishes."

He shifted to let her slide away, immediately regretting the loss of her warmth. "Dishwasher, at your service." He picked up the first bowl and turned on the sink as she went around the island to start putting away the ingredients they'd been using.

As he finished the last of the dishes, handing her the large bowl they'd made the filling in so she could dry it, the timer on the oven beeped gently.

"Think it's done?" he asked.

"Let's check." She set the bowl to the side and opened the oven, pulling on the mitt so she could jiggle the pie pans gently. "Looks set. Let's get them out."

"Want me to—"

Jess already had the first pie tin in her hands. She set it on a trivet she'd pulled out while he was doing the dishes and went back for the other one.

"Those smell amazing," he said.

"I know, right?" She grinned at him as she closed the oven with her heel. "How's that for something different?"

"It's certainly not apple fritters." He placed his face directly above the pies to inhale the fragrant steam rising from the warm filling. "I may die before they're cool enough to taste."

"I'm pretty sure you'll survive," she said dryly. "Tell me about your friends, the ones we're making these for."

He turned and leaned against the counter to look at her. "Now I feel like I'm taking advantage of you."

"What do you mean?"

"You're helping me make dessert for people you haven't even met, and I don't think I can just bring you with me tomorrow night."

She held up a hand. "Whoa, there."

He stopped. "Whoa?"

"First of all, I'm busy tomorrow night, thanks for asking." He winced at her tone. He wasn't winning any points tonight. Where had smooth Sean gone? Down the drain with the alcohol, apparently. Who knew he'd turn out to be so awkward? Jess was certainly finding out quickly, that was for sure. "Second, we barely know each other. I don't know how you usually do things—" *Ouch.* Point, hers. "—but let's just, you know, take it slow. Okay?" She looked up at him, lips thinned but eyes patient.

He took a deep breath. "Yes. Okay. I'm sorry. You're totally right. I'm not usually… I don't know."

"Inviting girls to meet your friends at the drop of a hat?"

"My friends have never even met any of the g—"

"Can you just… not finish that sentence?" Jess closed her eyes. "It's pretty unflattering for both of us."

He leaned forward and put his head in his hands, resting his elbows on the island countertop. "Oh, my God. I'm the worst."

She chuckled—a warm sound that moved through his body like he'd just drunk hot cocoa in a snowstorm. "Not even close to the worst, trust me. But yeah, you're not exactly batting a thousand, here."

"Want to start over?" He looked up at her hopefully.

"Nope. I want to cut into that." She pointed at the pie.

"That works."

They took small plates with slices of pie on them into the living room, and Sean closed his eyes after the first bite. "This is really good." He opened his eyes and inhaled most of the rest of the slice. It tasted a lot like the mole sauce he'd had at a tiny restaurant in L.A., but somehow also like a chocolate cream pie. "Insanely good."

"I know," Jess said. She'd eaten what appeared to be three small bites and set the rest aside. Before he could say anything, she smiled shyly up at him, and most of his thoughts vanished into the ball of want building in his gut. "Want to continue our conversation from before?"

"The one about how I'm the worst?"

She grinned shyly at him over the edge of his pie plate. "Not quite."

He set his empty plate down. "Is it—earlier, should I not have...?" He trailed off, suddenly unsure of what he was asking or how he should ask it.

"Kissed me?"

He nodded. "You stopped me."

She winced. "I did."

"Did you not want—"

"No, no, I did! You took me by surprise, and I just..." She stopped and looked up at him, warmth in her eyes. "I do like the idea of kissing you." She shrugged one shoulder as she held his gaze, a liquid movement that made Sean's entire body go hot and then cold.

He leaned towards her, shifting so that their bodies aligned on the couch. "May I kiss you now?"

She nodded, and he let his hands drift into her glorious hair before pulling her gently towards him. He couldn't remember feeling so tentative before. He didn't want to hurt her or make her angry—he had no idea what type of guy he was now. What if he wasn't good enough for her?

Their mouths met, and Sean let his worries slip away. She was sticky and sweet from the pie, and he let his lips roam around hers, gently licking his way in. She tasted like peace, and he craved it more than he'd ever imagined he would.

CHAPTER 8

*J*ess sipped her coffee as she waited for Marisol to walk through the door of The Hollow Bean. Unsurprisingly, her sister was late. What *was* surprising, though, was the fact that it had been Marisol who'd request they meet up this morning. Jess wasn't typically a suspicious person, but with the way Marisol had been acting toward her lately, she could only surmise her sibling wanted something.

Briefly, Jess's eyes fell to the small bag at her feet. Just in case, she'd brought samples of a new nail polish line, a charcoal face mask, and a candle made with essential oils that were supposed to calm you down.

A commotion on the other side of the room drew Jess's gaze. She winced as she watched her sister muscle her way through the crowd, knocking into fellow customers without stopping to apologize. True, the tables in The Hollow Bean were arranged awkwardly due to a fireplace that bisected the middle of the room, but regardless, her sister's disregard for others was rude. *That's just Marisol,* Jess mused. Lord knew she'd been subjected to similar behavior her entire life.

With a dramatic sigh, Marisol dropped down into the seat across from Jess and eyed the coffee in her hand expectantly. "You didn't order me anything?"

No hello. No how are you? Nothing.

Selfish and rude, Jess sighed inwardly. *As usual.* She kept hoping for something new, and Marisol never changed.

"I didn't know when you were getting here, and I knew you'd complain if your coffee was cold."

Marisol rolled her eyes. "I said I'd be here at ten." She raised her arm and glanced down at the watch on her wrist, a gift from their mother when Marisol had graduated from high school. "It's only ten-oh-five."

As subtly as she could, Jess dragged her left hand to the edge of the table and dropped it down into her lap. If Marisol saw her new Apple watch, she'd make a snide comment about it, and Jess didn't much feel like fighting with her sister this morning. She was still floating on cloud nine from her date the night before with Sean.

And yet …

"You said you'd be here at nine-thirty, which I figured meant ten."

"You're crazy," Marisol said, looking around for a waitress, even though she should know by now The Hollow Bean didn't have any waitstaff. They'd lived close to River Hill their entire lives.

Jess sighed with resignation. "Do you want me to show you the text you sent, or will you take my word for it that I can read?"

Marisol reached into her purse and grabbed her phone. Jess watched her sister pull up their string of messages and knew the moment Marisol realized Jess was telling the truth. She dropped her phone back into her bag and turned to hang it on the back of her chair. "Okay, fine. I'm a few minutes late."

Jess knew it was the only concession she was going to get, so she accepted it with a tight smile and decided to drop it. "So, what's up?" Jess asked over the rim of her mug.

Marisol's eyes flicked away guiltily as she launched into a story about Jason Junior needing something for school. Jess eventually stopped paying attention, and instead let her mind wander to everything she needed to get done that day, including putting together a video about a new henna dye her friend had used to disastrous effects. People really needed to know you should never use henna to color over hair that had been previously treated with dyes that contained metallic salts. The beauty industry might call them "shimmer agents," but she knew better.

She also figured she'd spend an hour or two sitting at her desk silently wondering if Sean was going to ask her out again. He'd kissed her last night—and quite thoroughly—so Jess was counting the night before as a date. Even if they hadn't explicitly called it that.

Now, just thinking about the way Sean had cradled her face in his large palms, and the gentle way he'd sucked her tongue into his mouth, had her stomach pitching and rolling. Her temperature spiked, and Jess felt her face grow warm. She raised her cup of coffee to her lips as Marisol continued speaking, hoping her sister wouldn't notice the blush creeping up her neck to tint her cheeks a burnished shade of pink.

She and Sean hadn't even reached second base but kissing him had been the single hottest experience of her life to date —and that included all the sex she'd had over the years. Okay, so there hadn't been much sex to speak of lately, but still. When a kiss was more physically potent than making love with your college boyfriend, a girl could be forgiven for swooning.

Marisol snapped her fingers in front of Jess's face. "Earth to Jess! Are you listening to me?"

She snapped back to the present. "I'm sorry, what?"

Marisol huffed. "I was telling you about a fundraiser at the boys' school—"

"Right. Jason is selling something?"

Her sister rolled her eyes. "I don't know why I even bother."

Jess clenched her jaw and tried to go to her happy place. That usually meant envisioning floating down the river with her friends on a warm summer's day, a bottle of Corona in her hand. Unfortunately, most of her old friends had gotten married and were raising young families or had moved away, so experiences like that were few and far between these days. But with the memory of Sean's kiss still fresh in her mind, she thought she might be able to conjure a new happy place: the sofa in the living room of her cozy little cottage.

And yet, for all her attempts at recapturing the magic from the night before, with her sister glaring daggers at her and tapping her fingernails on the table in an irritating staccato beat, Jess failed to locate her inner Zen. Which really pissed her off. Couldn't a girl have at least one day to bask in the bliss of a potential new relationship? Couldn't her sister take five minutes to ask Jess how she was doing for once, instead of immediately launching into all the ways Jess needed to help her? Couldn't *someone* be happy for her?

All at once, Jess snapped. "You bother because you know I'll give you free stuff and you can pretend that you spent a fortune on it."

Marisol's mouth dropped open. "What's gotten into you?"

"Do you realize that you didn't even ask me how I'm doing when you sat down? That you *never* ask how I am?"

Marisol crossed her arms over her chest. "I did too."

"No," Jess said, pinning her with an angry glare. "You did

not. And you never do. Just once, it'd be nice to tell you how things are going for me, instead of worrying about all the ways I need to walk on eggshells so that I don't upset you with some perceived slight."

"Fine! How are you?" Marisol barked, unconcerned that her voice echoed off the rafters of the coffee shop.

Jess set her cup to the side, debating whether or not she even wanted Marisol to know how she was doing. Whether her sister would find some new and inventive way to skew all the successes in Jess's life into something that was somehow an indictment of the differences between them. But with girlfriends scarce these days, and a feeling of loneliness washing over her, she wished that she and Marisol had the type of sisterly relationship she'd read about. Perhaps she hadn't done enough herself to foster that. Maybe if she only tried a bit harder to connect with Marisol, things could be different.

Her voice gentling, Jess said, "I got a job offer. A good one."

Marisol's voice dropped a few octaves too. "Something stable?"

Jess let the implied meaning of the statement slide. "It could be. One of the morning shows I've been a guest on a few times wants to have me on regularly."

She hadn't worked out all the details with the station yet, but it sounded like they wanted to have her to do two segments a week for the next six months. If she proved popular with their audience, there was room to expand her contract. Jess didn't want to count her chickens before they hatched, but she knew how to connect with women in a way that made them feel good about themselves. The traffic on her blog didn't lie. Data was data, and it proved that Jess was good at what she did. And her latest angle—real talk about beauty—was clearly resonating. Whether or not that translated into success with a live studio audience remained to be seen, but she was confident.

"Ooh, is that the one you did the segment with last week?"

Jess tried to tamp down her surprise. "You watched?"

Marisol nodded. "I was getting the boys ready for school, and it was on in the background. When I heard your name, I turned the TV up."

Hearing that her sister had watched the segment thawed Jess's heart. With two rambunctious boys, it couldn't have been easy to get them out the door in the morning, but she'd set aside that time anyhow.

"It wasn't my best showing," Jess admitted, "but I think I turned it around in the end."

Marisol laughed. "You looked terrible." She reached for Jess's coffee and drained the last of it. Wiping her mouth with the back of her hand, she made a face. "Ugh, mocha. I'm surprised. Don't you need to watch your weight?"

Ouch.

There she was, the Marisol Jess knew and loved … despite her acerbic tongue.

"It's my one indulgence," Jess admitted as she stared longingly into her empty mug.

"Speaking of indulgences," Marisol said, bringing Jess's attention back to their conversation, "I have someone I want to set you up with."

"You *what?*" Jess glanced around the coffee shop to make sure there weren't any hidden cameras. Marisol had *never* tried to set her up with anyone. Mostly because she thought Jess was a stuck-up, no-fun, goody-two-shoes who couldn't hold onto a man if her life depended on it. Jess had never had the proverbial balls to point out to her sister that Marisol was the one who'd been cheated on several times. She liked her hair way too much to do something that would result in a bald patch once her sister yanked a chunk of it out.

Marisol leaned closer. "I saw that segment, Jess. You're beautiful, but you've lost your glow. You look like you need to get laid." She beamed beatifically at her sister as though she'd delivered advice from the heavens.

Jess's jaw dropped open. "I ... My ... How ..." she sputtered, at a loss for words.

And just like that, her mind flashed back to the night before.

To the hungry look on Sean's face as he'd eyed her bending over to fetch the pies from the oven. To the way he'd hummed low in the back of his throat as his tongue had licked its way inside her mouth. He'd tasted like chocolate and spice, like something decadent and forbidden. Jess clamped her thighs together to try and control the pulse beating in her core.

"I'm seeing someone," she blurted.

"Really?" Marisol asked, her eyebrow raised in disbelief. "Then how come you look like you haven't been fucked properly in years?" She cackled at her own joke.

For her part, Jess didn't see anything funny about it at all.

The truth was, she *hadn't* been fucked. Properly, or *ever* for that matter.

Just thinking the word had her squirming—and not necessarily in a good way. She didn't *fuck*. She had sex. Or made love. Jess didn't know what she would do if things got so hot and heavy that a man resorted to using words like that with her. No one in the history of ever had been so turned on that they'd looked at her and said something as brazen as "Get on the bed so I can fuck you."

The thought of it was faintly nauseating.

And yet, she couldn't deny that her pulse rocketed when she imagined Sean talking dirty to her. Telling her all the ways he wanted to be with her, his hips rolling against hers as he grunted out his release.

Abruptly, Jess pushed back from her chair and stood. "I have to go."

The last thing she heard as she practically ran out of the Hollow Bean was Marisol's knowing laugh.

CHAPTER 9

Sean slid the last tray of croissants into the top rack of the glass-fronted display case. He'd flown through prep this morning like his whole body was energized from his evening with Jess. He could feel a smile curve across his face as he thought about the way she'd felt in his arms. She'd been the full five-senses experience—every single one exceptional, from taste to touch. How soon would be too soon to call her again? The smile faded as he realized he had no idea how to date somebody.

His gaze fell on the messenger bag he usually carried to work—he typically hauled a cookbook or two around with him, plus a printout of the bakery's annual budget, which he was trying to learn to decipher. Today, it held the remaining spices from the pie waiting for him in the fridge at home. He'd forgotten to take them out when he'd tossed them in there after he'd left Jess's house the night before. He reached in and found the bottle of cinnamon, flipping it over in his hands. A word on the opposite side of the label stood out to his primed eye: 'cookies.'

"Cookies, huh?" He squinted at the bottle, noting that it

directed readers to visit the company's website for their recipe for Mexican Wedding Cookies. Girls liked cookies, right? Maybe he'd make some for Jess. And some extras for Noah and Angelica. He pulled out his phone and tapped in the website address.

Forty minutes later, the rich scent of cinnamon and walnuts mixed with all the other delicious smells of the bakery as he pulled two trays of little round cookies out of the oven. He slid them onto the counter to cool while he pulled out confectioner's sugar to dust them with.

"Those smell incredible," somebody said behind him.

He turned and realized he had a customer—the man must have come in while Sean was busy with the oven. "How's it going, Mr. Hughes?"

"Spectacular, as always," the older man said. "Are those ready?" He pointed at the trays on the counter. "I'll take three if they are."

Sean blinked. "I … uh …"

"I can wait a couple of minutes."

"They're—"

"Oh, and my usual two croissants, too. Can't go home without them." Mr. Hughes chuckled.

Sean's hands were moving without his conscious direction, pulling out and bagging the croissants before he'd even registered he was doing it. He looked back at the cookies, then at the other man's hopeful expression. He thought briefly of his mother, her shelves of cookbooks, and the conversation they'd had. The one where she'd told him in no uncertain terms that he was never to deviate from the family's beloved recipes. His eyebrows snapped down. "Coming right up," he said, knowing he'd pay for this small act of rebellion later. The punishment would be worth it.

He slid three cookies through the waiting powdered sugar, tapped them twice to get rid of the excess, and then popped them into the smallest bag he had behind the counter. Then he did some swift mental math to come up with a price. Or rather, three prices—one cookie, half a dozen, and a dozen, based on the pricing the bakery already used for the other kinds of cookies they sold. Those treats weren't something they kept on hand every day— The Breadery was generally more of a pastry operation— but he'd made plenty of batches of holiday cookies in his time.

He ran Mr. Hughes's credit card and sent the man on his way with a smile and a wave. Then he took a deep breath and thought about what he'd just done. The rest of the cookies sat waiting on their trays, staring back at him in pale, lumpy expectancy. They would sell. They smelled incredible. But his mother had been more than clear. The Breadery had a standard operating plan, and he wasn't supposed to deviate from it. He didn't have the right to deviate from it, since he wasn't the person he was pretending to be. He wasn't the prodigal son, River Hill's darling returned home. He was a wreck. He was broken, and he didn't know where he belonged.

But the cookies were good. And the customers wanted them. He swallowed his doubts and sold a dozen more to the next person who came in—noting that they still purchased the items they'd initially come in for, too, just like Mr. Hughes had. After they left, he ate one himself. The buttery confection crumbled on his tongue, coating his mouth in rich sugar and cinnamon. It was delicious. Briefly, he wondered if Jess would like them.

Then he remembered her strange reaction to the pie they'd made and wondered if she would even eat them. Did she not like sweets? He shook his head. She'd said she loved the pie; it was the reason she'd thought of it when he'd confessed his need for something new. He'd have to ask her when he saw her next. And just in case, not mention the cookies.

The door opened again while he was contemplating this, and he looked up to see Maeve Brennan entering the bakery. His face relaxed into a real smile. "Hi, Maeve."

Iain Brennan's younger sister grinned at him, her mouth wide over a pointed chin that made her occasionally resemble a pixie. Her red hair was up in a messy bun, and she was wearing a gray t-shirt with the logo of the distillery she and her brother owned blazoned across the chest. "Hey, Sean. I need sustenance. Of the baked variety."

"Rough day?"

"Phone call with my da," she said, her Irish accent coming through strongly. Maeve had moved to River Hill shortly after Iain had last year, joining her brother in the distilling venture. Their family was whiskey royalty back in Ireland, but the two youngest Brennans had wanted to do something different from the classic whiskey they'd grown up producing. Their family had resisted—especially after Iain had met Naomi, who wasn't exactly a model of stability and traditional values.

Sean liked the famed artist a lot, and she was one of Noah's best friends, but she'd been resisting her own high-society family's efforts to set her up with a doctor for so long that she'd practically made a career of one-night-stands. Just like Sean, if he was honest with himself. Although, as he understood it, she'd had much better reasons.

He hadn't been privy to all the details of what had happened, but at some point last year, the Brennans and the Kleins had all descended on River Hill at once. Angelica still laughed every time she talked about it. In the end, Iain and Naomi had moved in together, Maeve had gotten a place nearby, and the distillery was starting to do a brisk business.

He'd tried it back when he was still drinking. It was delicious.

Maeve and Iain were both working their butts off to make the business work, and he respected them for it. "What can I get for you?"

Her eyes drifted to the cookies, now tucked into a basket on the counter. "Some of those? They smell amazing. I've never seen you selling them before. Are they new?"

If there was anybody who'd understand what he'd just done, it was Maeve. "Brand new. And, uh, unauthorized."

Her eyebrows went up, and she leaned forward. "Do tell."

"I might be slightly going against orders from the owner," he confessed.

"The owner being your mum, right?" Maeve quirked her head to the side and grinned. "You rebel." Then she looked startled at her own words. "I mean— sorry! Not trying to say it's a bad thing." She frowned. "Or a good thing?" She looked up at him. "It's whatever kind of thing you think it should be!"

Sean laughed. He'd forgotten the thing that they'd all discovered about Maeve when she'd joined his group of friends: she was tough and stubborn, but she was also the single nicest person on the planet. How she'd managed to stand up to the kind of conflict Iain had described regarding his father's attitude about their 'desertion' was beyond Sean's imagining. He had mad respect for her.

"I'll take it as a good thing, at least for now." He shrugged. "The customers seem to like them, so I can at least tell her we're making money off of them." He wasn't relishing the conversation he was going to have to have with his mother, even though he believed he was right.

Maeve nodded. "Family can be hard. And going against their wishes can be even harder. They want what they think is best for you and the business, and it can be challenging to disagree."

"Is it worth it?"

She smiled. "Definitely."

* * *

"THIS IS NEW." Noah slipped the foil off of the top of the pie and stared at it, then looked up at Sean. "Pie?"

"Special pie," Sean clarified. He leaned back in his chair and smirked at his friend.

"There had better not be any weed in that pie," Angelica called from the kitchen. A clatter announced that she'd dumped the stack of dirty plates she'd been carrying into the sink. Noah's house—his and Angelica's house, really, these days—was mostly an open floor plan, but the dining room was separated from the kitchen by a small section of wall. Presumably so guests wouldn't see the mess Angelica made when she cooked.

"Not that kind of special," Sean said. "When was the last time you even had that kind of thing?"

Angelica returned to the dining room, drying her hands on a kitchen towel and looking thoughtful. "It's not really my scene," she said. "I tried it a few times at parties in Hollywood."

"I'm a booze guy," Noah said. "Never bothered."

"And yet you assumed that I'd bring you a pot pie? Pun not strictly intended," he added as they both snickered. "Thanks."

"You're just our fun, unpredictable friend," Angelica offered with a placating smile.

"I'm not that bad," he grumbled.

"Not anymore, anyway," Noah said. "What's in the pie?"

"Chocolate and a bunch of really cool spices, plus pepitas and some dried chilies."

"Chilies in a pie?" Noah narrowed his eyes. "Who are you, and what have you done with Sean?"

"First you call me unpredictable, and now you're saying I never do anything different?" Sean tried to make a joke of it, but much as he appreciated his friends' intervention in his drinking, their opinion of him was starting to rankle.

"You were unpredictable in other ways," Noah said. "We just didn't know you'd taken to kitchen experimentation. I've never seen The Breadery sell anything like this, and I've lived in River Hill for more than ten years." He gestured toward the pie.

Sean shrugged. "I thought I'd try something new. Not everyone wants to stay in a rut." He glanced toward his friends, letting a wicked glimmer enter his eyes. "Speaking of ruts, are you two ever going to get married?"

Angelica held up her hands. "Whoa, whoa, Mister Unpredictable, you don't get to turn this around on us!" She glanced up at her fiancé, her face softening into familiar fondness. "Noah and I are just fine." She leveled a finger at him. "Nice try."

Sean raised his eyebrow at Noah, who winced. "Just fine, huh? You finally give up, old man?" Noah had been trying to persuade his busy fiancée to tie the knot for almost two years now. Her career as an in-demand personality on RenoTV, the home renovation network, plus her popular B&B next door to Noah's house kept her either filming or working what seemed like nonstop. Sean wasn't sure why she couldn't just get married and keep doing the same thing, but her frenetic pace didn't seem to leave enough time to plan a wedding. Noah had once confessed that they both wanted kids, but Angelica wasn't quite ready yet. Sean wondered if she was trying to cram her whole career in now, just in case things changed in a way she didn't expect once they finally did have children. He couldn't really blame her.

"I haven't given up," Noah said. "I'm strategizing." He grinned at Angelica and twirled a lock of her blonde hair around one of his fingers. "We'll get there."

She smiled up at him, then turned a determined gaze to Sean. "So then, what's up with you?"

"Um, nothing?" He loved both of them dearly. Noah was one of his best friends. But occasionally he wished his friend had fallen in love with somebody a little less… involved.

Although, to be fair, it wasn't like Noah himself wasn't just as bad. Like now, when the big winemaker leaned forward with a skeptical twist of his lips. "Something's going on with you. Tell us. I'll cut the pie." He lifted a knife and nodded at Sean.

Sean sighed. Might as well. "I've been thinking about the bakery and my future."

"Whoa. Heavy." Noah slid a piece of pie his way as Angelica handed him a dessert fork.

"Thanks." He took a bite of the pie, the flavors on his tongue reminding him of Jess, and when he'd licked chocolate off her lips as they lay tangled up in each other on her couch. He blinked away the memory. "I guess I just want to start thinking about where I'm going."

"Are you going somewhere?" Angelica frowned and took a bite of pie. "Oh, my god. This is amazing."

"I don't know. I always thought I'd go back to L.A. eventually, go back to producing. But lately, I keep thinking about the bakery, and how we could change things."

Angelica raised one eyebrow. "Changing things? Have you talked to your mom about it?"

"Yeah. It didn't go well."

She nodded. "So what are you going to do?"

He winced. "I may have spontaneously sold a new product today."

"Well, that's committing to a cause," Angelica said. "Are you prepared for the fallout?"

"Not at all," he confessed. "But I'm going to have to deal with it anyway. Turns out that's what being an adult is, who knew?"

"Not that I'm not fully in support of any and all personal growth," Noah said. "But where did this come from? Feels like just a few weeks ago we were pulling your head out of a bottle, and now you're leaps and bounds ahead of just not drinking."

Angelica elbowed him. "We're proud of that," she said pointedly.

"I never said we weren't!" Noah protested. "I'm just curious."

Noah knew him a little too well, Sean realized. He sighed. "I did spend some time with a new friend, actually. She's the one who gave me the recipe for the pie." He didn't mention that they'd baked it together, but neither Noah nor Angelica was slow on the uptake. Their eyes narrowed simultaneously.

"Another one?" Angelica sounded disappointed.

Noah was more casual. "Anybody we know?"

"It's not like that," he snapped, startling himself with his response. Noah and Angelica exchanged a glance he couldn't interpret, some sort of couples telepathy he wasn't privy to. "Don't—" He drew in a steadying breath. *I don't think she deserves to be talked about that way. I don't think of her that way.* Jess definitely wasn't a one-night-stand. He wasn't entirely sure what she was, but he was damn sure that he wanted to see her again. Soon.

CHAPTER 10

*P*ulling a deep, fortifying breath into her lungs, Jess straightened her spine and squared her shoulders. *There's nothing to be nervous about,* she told herself as she pushed off the curb, putting one foot in front of the other as she made her way across the street and into the bakery.

She and Sean weren't exactly dating, but if their makeout session the week before was anything to go by, they were beyond just friends. And people who were more than friends did the pop-by-unexpectedly thing, didn't they? Of course, Marisol would have told her showing up where Sean worked was akin to stalking the man, but it had been a few days since she'd last seen him, and she was jonesing for more.

She'd never actually been inside The Breadery before, so she was somewhat surprised to see how utterly charming it was. Not that she'd been hanging out in bakeries much—not with her diet—but it was a lot homier than the panaderias on the other side of town. Its colorful decorations and vintage signs and photography made it look like something straight out of *Gilmore Girls.* Glancing around, Jess almost expected

Lorelai Gilmore to pop out any second, a giant mug of coffee clutched tight in her hands.

With a pang, Jess recalled all the times she'd stayed up late into the night binging the show with Marisol when they were younger. When its revival season had aired a couple of years ago, she'd hoped her sister would come over and watch it with her, but Marisol had scoffed and said she was too busy. It had seemed like a waste of time to point out that Marisol had just spent the previous twenty minutes talking Jess's ear off about some show featuring a time-traveling doctor and her eighteenth-century Scottish lover.

Jess pushed the memory of that conversation aside. She was here to see Sean, not take uncomfortable trips down Memory Lane.

Standing in line behind an elderly couple that was trying to decide what pastries to purchase, Jess let her eye wander to the photographs lining the wall, where one in particular caught her attention. She stared at it for a few brief seconds, making sure her eyes weren't deceiving her. Nope, they weren't. Once upon a time, the storefront of The Breadery had been painted white, and in big black letters, a sign hung over the door welcoming customers to Amory & Sons Bakery.

As in Sean Amory. As in her not-quite-boyfriend *owned* the place?

Jess's eyes narrowed in suspicion as her gaze bounced back to Sean. He was ringing up the couple, and it didn't seem as if he'd noticed her yet. While she was still incognito, Jess took a moment to study him. He looked better than he had when their paths had first crossed. His face had filled out somewhat, his cheekbones less gaunt than they'd been, and his eyes weren't as pinched as she remembered them being. During their first brief conversation, he'd been a bit green around the gills, but now his skin positively glowed with vitality and good health. His hair was still overly long and shaggy, and she wasn't sure if he was trying to grow a beard or if he just hadn't bothered shaving—his scruff was in that in-between stage that could go either way—but he looked *good*.

As Jess continued observing him interacting with his customers, she wasn't sure why she was so bothered by learning that he owned the bakery. Mostly, she realized, it was that he hadn't told her. While they'd spoken by phone a few times and had exchanged several text messages, she was coming to realize that he was cautious with his words. Now, she wondered if he purposefully kept things from her. Not that owning one of the most successful businesses in River Hill made a difference to her one way or the other. It was the principle of the thing.

Then again, she'd done the same thing, hadn't she? Or had she? She wasn't sure that not telling the guy you were crushing on that you'd been on a diet since you'd hit puberty was the same thing as not telling the woman you'd kissed senseless that you owned a highly-respected local business.

She didn't have too long to mull it over, though. Their transaction complete, the older couple moved aside, and Sean crouched down to inspect his inventory.

Jess stepped forward to take their place at the counter.

"What can I get you?" His voice was muffled from his position below the edge of the counter.

"What's good?" Jess asked, pushing aside her misgivings about the puzzle that was Sean Amory. Not that she had any intention of eating whatever he recommended. She'd take it to her papa later, she decided.

Sean pushed to his feet, a shy grin splitting his lips as his eyes landed on Jess. "Hey, you."

Jess fluttered her fingers in greeting. "How's it going?"

"Good. Yourself?" He leaned forward, propping his forearms on the counter.

Jess hadn't noticed it before, but Sean's arms were enticingly muscular, his skin dusted with golden hair that shimmered in the sunlight that streamed in through the windows at the front of the shop. She licked her lips, wondering briefly what his skin would taste like if she were to lean down and lick a path over the vein that ran the length of his inner arm.

She shook her head, banishing the ridiculous thought, and raised her eyes to his as she gestured over her shoulder to where her car was parked on the other side of the street. "I was in the neighborhood and decided to pop in. I hope that's okay."

"Far be it from me to complain when a beautiful woman stops in to see me." Sean pushed off the counter and flashed her a flirty smile filled with so much smoldering heat that it rendered Jess momentarily speechless.

She'd seen a few flashes of *this* guy before—the smooth talker, the ladies' man, the guy who'd run circles around her if she let him—but she'd come to think of Sean as a nice guy. Maybe even a bit vulnerable. The look on his face right now, though? She got the distinct impression that this man was a wolf in sheep's clothing. Briefly, she wondered if she was in over her head.

She glanced away nervously, and her eyes connected with the black and white photo that had caught her earlier attention. She cleared her throat and brought her gaze back to his. "I didn't realize you owned this place."

Sean gripped the back of his neck as his face dropped forward an inch. Looking up at Jess, he said, "I don't. Not really."

Reflexively, she crossed her arms over her chest and notched her head toward the wall where the framed photo resided. "So that's not your name on that picture over there?"

Sean lifted his apron off over his head and stepped out from behind the counter, dropping the bunched fabric on the white and gray marble as he went. When he reached her side, he set his hand on her upper back and gently ushered her toward the wall lined with faded photographs. Pointing at one toward the top, he said, "That's my great-great-grandfather, Thomas Amory." He gestured at another sepia-toned photo. "And that's my grandfather Thomas, Jr., his oldest son. He took the bakery over when his father passed." He led her a bit further down, pointing at a third photo, this one in faded color. "And that's my dad and my mom. My grandpa didn't have any sons, so the bakery went to her. She's the one who changed the name to The Breadery. She and my dad planned to run it together forever, but ..." He trailed off, and his eyes flashed with agony.

All at once, Jess felt *very* uncomfortable. She hadn't meant to force him to talk about something that was so obviously painful. She laid a comforting hand to his arm. "It's okay; you don't have to explain."

"I think I do, though." He shrugged out from her touch and faced the wall of photos, crossing his arms over his chest. "I never planned on working here. My parents were so solid. It seemed like they'd be here, running things, forever and ever. So I went to college, chose a career. I thought that if and when they retired, the place would go to one of the Amory cousins. But then my dad died. And I didn't come home, and my mom didn't hand off the bakery to anyone, just kept running things by herself. And then when things fell apart for me down in Southern California ... well, here I am." He glanced at her out of the corner of his eye as he finished speaking.

"I'm sorry," Jess whispered. She tried to imagine his

mother losing a beloved partner and couldn't. It would be like her abuela without her papa. Inconceivable. "Thanks," he said, turning on his heels and moving back behind the counter. "With him gone and my mom getting older, it made sense for me to come home and help out where I could. The truth is, I'm more of an employee than anything else."

Jess detected a note of bitterness in his response. "How so?" she asked, canting her head to the side to study his reactions. Every so often she detected something troubled simmering just below the surface. This was one of those times, and she wasn't entirely convinced it had to do with the passing of his father. The way he'd just spoken—the tone of his voice and the clipped cadence of speech—made her think he felt deeply dissatisfied with how his life had played out. A feeling she was familiar with, Jess thought ruefully.

"For starters—" he turned around and futzed with a sheet pan of cherry tarts "—I don't really get a say in how the business is run. I just open up each morning, bake what the chart tells me to, and pass it all off to the next schlub when I leave." He glanced at her over his shoulder before moving to the rear of the storefront and tossing his apron on a peg on the far wall. When he returned to the counter, his shoulders were tight, and that pinched look was back in his eyes.

His reaction confirmed her earlier suspicions. Sean was *not* happy with the current state of his life. Briefly, Jess wondered if that's why he'd been so reluctant to reveal much about himself. Now probably wasn't the time to broach the subject, and yet ...

"You told me once before that you used to work in the entertainment industry, but I don't know much beyond that." It wasn't a question so much as a statement, but she hoped he'd pick up the reins of the conversation and fill in her blanks.

He didn't. Instead, he stared at her for a few beats and

then blew out a breath, his gaze darting away. "Yeah, I don't like to talk about it."

Jess tried not to dwell on the disappointment his non-answer evoked. Things were still so new between them, she told herself. It was crazy to expect him to spill all his secrets in one fell swoop. Besides, she reasoned, him confessing his sad family history was a massive step in their relationship. They had plenty of time to learn all each other's secrets. Assuming, of course, he was as into her as she was into him. Sometimes, like now, she couldn't be sure.

"Anyhow," he said, running his hand through his messy hair, "I'm done here for the day." He looked pointedly toward the door, and Jess realized he was hoping she'd leave.

Okay. So Sean isn't into me, she thought with a lurch of her hopeful heart.

But then he stepped around the counter and came to stand in front of her. "Want to get dinner with me tomorrow night, and we can talk more?"

All at once, Jess's hope spiked. She looked up into his deep blue eyes and their gazes locked. It was apparent Sean was battling some unspoken demons, but she wanted to *know* him. Know all about those demons, and maybe … just maybe … help him conquer them. She couldn't say why, but she felt deep into the marrow of her bones that they had a connection, tenuous though it might be. So even though she knew there was a very good possibility that he could break her heart, she let that hope soar. "That sounds great."

CHAPTER 11

Sean wasn't proud of the way he'd smoothly deflected Jess's line of questioning yesterday. He squirmed a little in the driver's seat as he recalled her look of disappointment when he'd practically shoved her out the door of the bakery. But there was only so much talk about his family and his past that he could handle in broad daylight, at work, in front of God and croissants.

When he'd blurted out his invitation to dinner, he'd thought he would take her to Frankie's for some of Max's incredible cooking. But this morning during his shift, he'd remembered how taken aback she'd been by the revelation that his family owned The Breadery. Maybe meeting his pile of overly inquisitive and unnecessarily helpful friends wasn't the greatest idea, not yet. No matter how many punctuation marks Noah and Angelica added to the increasingly frequent texts they were sending him.

He hadn't been keeping secrets from her, exactly; they just didn't know each other that well yet. He winced as he pulled Bessie Blue to a halt in front of her house. That wasn't entirely true. He had no intention of talking to her about what had happened in L.A. So maybe he *was* keeping secrets. But she was the girl he was hoping to get naked, not his therapist. Not that he had a therapist. He did have the business card Noah had given him still, though. Not throwing it away had to be considered progress, right?

All thoughts of therapy—and pretty much everything else — vanished from his head when Jess opened the door. He'd texted and told her to dress for the city, which she clearly understood. *Wow.* Her lean curves were draped in a dress that clung everywhere, in a shade of deep red that matched her lip color and showed off that glowing skin he'd admired so much when she'd jogged past the bakery. Her dark hair was swept up in loose waves, held up by some woven contraption that glimmered with a hint of crystal in the darkening twilight.

"You look amazing," he told her when he reached the front porch.

"Thanks," she said quietly. "You look great, too."

He shrugged, feeling awkward as the fabric of his suit slid against his shoulders. He'd pulled one of his old ones from the back of his closet—one of the designers he'd worn every day back in his former, fashionable life. He hadn't realized how much a year or two of alternating between drinking and working his butt off would change the shape of his body. He'd put some weight back on since he'd quit drinking, but nothing fit quite the way it used to. If Jess liked what she saw, however, he wasn't going to correct her. "Ready?"

She nodded, and he took her arm to escort her to the truck. She giggled as she approached it. "Where are we going?"

"A place in San Francisco," he said.

"When you told me to dress for the city, I didn't think you'd be driving this," she said, patting the side of the truck as she slipped carefully into the passenger seat, giving her dress a quick tug as she sat so it would stay smooth.

He shut the door for her and crossed over to his seat. "I *did* think about borrowing something else, but I couldn't decide which seemed more awkward: showing up in a vintage truck or showing up in my mom's car."

She laughed. "I think you probably made the right choice."

"Everybody loves old Bessie Blue," he said smugly. He gave the steering wheel a gentle pat as he started the truck, enjoying her signature rumble.

"I hope the valet does, too."

He glanced over and realized she was looking back at him with a sly smile. He snorted. "What, you don't think fancy restaurants see people pulling up in these babies all the time?"

"I'm sure they do."

"She's practically one of a kind, I'll have you know."

"She's beautiful," Jess soothed.

The forty-minute drive passed quickly as they chatted about their weeks at work, what they wanted to do for their next vacations, and names they liked for pets they'd never had and likely never would.

"I always thought I'd name an iguana Ignatius," Sean said as he pulled Bessie Blue to a stop outside La Panneau.

"Like the saint?" Jess nodded to the valet, who opened her door for her.

"More like just cool alliteration." When he reached Jess's side, he handed the keys to the valet, who stared at him and then at the truck. "I know, buddy, she's beautiful. Don't scratch her." He leaned toward Jess as the valet walked around the car. "You're beautiful, too."

"Am I competing with a truck?" she teased.

"You'd win," he said, his eyes raking over her one more

time in appreciation before they went inside and he lost half of her under the table. His old job had made him a fixture of the Hollywood scene, so he'd been with his fair share of beautiful women over the years—each one blonder and thinner than the next, it had seemed. And yet, he realized with no small amount of surprise, none of them had held a candle to the beauty at his side. There was simply no measuring up to the effortless grace of Jessica Casillas-Moore.

"What a relief," she answered with a shy smile as they made their way inside.

They stepped to the podium, and Sean gave the host his name. Reservations at La Panneau were notoriously hard to come by, but he'd traded on a couple of old contacts to get a table, feeling a bit of a pang as he did. It was like dipping his toe back into dangerous waters. But he had to start somewhere, right? And with Jess by his side, radiating whatever it was that she did that was so soothing, he could handle it. Probably.

After they were seated, Jess picked up her menu as a waitress arrived to take their drink orders. After she ordered sparkling water, Jess glanced over at him. "Did you want the wine list?"

He let the familiar thirst wash over him and shook his head. "No, I'm good, thanks. I'll stick with the same." The waitress nodded and vanished.

Jess smiled. "You are driving, after all."

"Yep, something like that." He was getting better at ignoring the itch under his tongue that offers of alcohol seemed to produce every time they came his way. It was easy to ignore it here, with Jess to distract him. It would be much harder in L.A., he reflected. Assuming, of course, he ever went back. He shook his head. Why on earth was he thinking about this now?

Jess was perusing her menu. "I think I'll get the tuna."

"Sounds good," he said. "I'll get that, too."

"Ugh, no, you can't," she protested. "I can't get the same thing as you! How will we maximize the number of things we're trying?" She lifted her menu again. "I'll pick something else."

"No, no." He reached out a hand to push her menu back to the table. "I will." He chuckled. "I didn't know we had to maximize anything. I'll get the chicken."

She looked adorably embarrassed. "I'm sorry. I just hate to duplicate food at a restaurant, since the whole point of going to one is to eat food you wouldn't at home."

"I'm not sure I've ever thought of going to a restaurant that way."

"Why, how do you think of it?"

"As, um, a place to eat?"

She laughed. "You don't do much in the way of home cooking, do you?"

Before he could shake his head, the waitress came back to take their orders and hand over their drinks. He enjoyed watching Jess order her food, something he didn't expect. She was so animated, and her enjoyment of the evening seeped into him, soothing the restlessness that so often consumed him.

"So?" She turned to him as the waitress left again.

"Hm?" He'd been distracted by watching the play of her shoulder blades as her hair drifted against them.

"Cooking. You. Not much?" She exaggerated her words patiently, making him chuckle.

"Not really. I've always been more of a baking guy. I can cook, I guess—my mom made sure I'd be able to feed myself before I left for college. But it turns out I'm fundamentally lazy."

"The guy who's working at four o'clock in the morning is

lazy? I thought my early morning jogs were some kind of virtuous martyrdom, but you're taking the cake, baker boy." She paused. "Pun not entirely intended but appreciated nonetheless."

He laughed. "That's work. I set myself a schedule, and I do it. Just because my work involves producing food doesn't mean I'm at home cooking up gourmet fare."

"Please tell me you don't survive on Hamburger Helper," she said.

"No, I usually go out," he said. "There's a restaurant in River Hill named Frankie's. Have you been there?"

She shook her head. "I don't eat out a ton, honestly."

"A friend of mine owns it, so I eat there quite a bit." He glanced around, once again comparing this quiet, overly elegant place to the flushed charm of Frankie's. "You should try it."

"So why didn't we go there? Why all this?" She flicked her hand in a circle, somehow encompassing the entire restaurant, from the gentle tinkle of silverware against plates to the murmur of conversation hushed by expensive tailoring and plush carpets. It was a far cry from the cheerful noise that imbued Frankie's. The waitress hadn't even rolled her eyes at him once. He hadn't expected to miss that.

"Maybe I was trying to impress you," he said.

She chuckled, warm and low in her throat, making his groin tighten. "You don't need to do that. I've seen you with dish soap on your nose."

He laughed. "You're right. Honestly, I just thought… maybe we needed some privacy before we plunge in. See where this is going, make sure we really like each other enough to be teased by friends and family for hours on end." He attempted his best smooth-charmer smile, hoping it didn't come out as lopsided as it felt. The thought of his friends ribbing him about her made him inexplicably restless.

She pursed her lips thoughtfully. "You know, I can't say I disagree with you." She raised her eyebrows, then smiled at him a little shyly. "I do like whatever this is we've got going on. And I love River Hill, but it's a gossip farm, isn't it?"

He snorted. "You've got that right."

When Angelica had started dating Noah, she'd confessed once that it had seemed like the entire town had taken pains to pointedly remind her that he'd once been seen leaving Naomi's house early in the morning. Since the two women were close friends, Angelica had been well aware of her fiancé's prior relationship—if you could call it that—with the artist and hadn't particularly minded. What she *hadn't* enjoyed was having the bulk of the town council asking her intrusive questions about it during a meeting of the tourism board.

"So. We have privacy to get to know each other?" She grinned. "What's your favorite color?"

"Blue. You?"

"Red. Most of the time."

"Most of the time? You're a fickle favoriter?" He tsked. "I thought better of you."

She laughed. "Sometimes I'm just not in a red mood!"

He shook his head in mock sadness as their entrees arrived, barely noticing the waiter who placed them on the table and whisked silently away. Their conversation flowed smoothly through dinner—like they'd known each other for years but still had so much to discover about one another. He was holding back, though. He couldn't bring himself to tell her about Cal's death. It was in the past; it was over. That said, he owed it to her to tell her about the drinking. If he wanted this relationship to continue—if he wanted to have more dinner dates where she didn't ask him if he wanted the wine list—he needed to say something, and soon. Hell, if nothing else, she deserved to know she was starting something up with a man who had alcoholic tendencies.

Inwardly, Sean shuddered. He'd skated around the word for months now, but as he considered how to talk to Jess about his problem, he was forced to acknowledge the truth: he was very likely an alcoholic.

He didn't get up the nerve to broach the subject until they were nearly back to River Hill. As Bessie Blue crested one of the gently rolling hills that led into town from the river, he slowed the truck and pulled off onto a gravel road. It was one of the back entrances to Noah's vineyard, and there was a small parking area set back from the main road that his workers sometimes used when they were in this section of vines. He parked Bessie close to the edge of the cleared area, letting the vines drape over truck like a curtain of privacy.

"What's up?" Jess asked, her brow furrowed slightly. She masked her obvious concern by going for a light joke. "I feel fairly confident you're not going to murder me in a vineyard. I could be wrong, though."

"No murder agenda tonight," he said. "I just wanted to tell you something." Her eyes widened, and he held up a hand. "Don't freak out! I'm not declaring my undying love!" *Not yet,* a tiny voice in his head whispered. "I just wanted to talk to you about, um, my drinking."

She blinked. "I haven't seen you drink anything but water."

"Yeah. I guess I'm, uh, recovering? I used to drink a lot. Too much." It was the first time he'd admitted out loud that he'd had a problem. It felt like exhaling for too long. Strange, breathless.

Her mouth formed an O, and her eyes flicked up and down his body. He felt himself flush. "I'd just stopped drinking when you and I first met. It hasn't been long."

"You look … better," she said quietly.

"I feel better. But it's still pretty hard."

Her hand flew to her mouth. "Oh, no, and I asked you about the wine list! Sean, I'm so sorry!" She looked so genuinely distressed that he wanted to hug her.

"It's okay." He reached out to take her hand, tugging it away from her face and twining his fingers into hers. "It's my own fault for not telling you. I should have said something."

Her eyes were troubled, and he didn't know what else he could say. So he gave in to what he'd wanted to do since she'd opened her front door. He leaned forward and kissed her.

CHAPTER 12

*J*ess hadn't seen Sean's kiss coming. One minute they were talking about his drinking problem, and the next he was moving toward her, his eyes dark and hungry in the reflective glow of the dash. And then his mouth was on hers, and it was the most heartbreakingly sweet kiss she'd ever experienced. Slow and careful, his lips caressing hers hesitantly but thoroughly—as if he wasn't sure what he was doing, but wild horses couldn't have kept him away.

Jess knew they needed to have a good long talk about … well, everything. But she also needed her toes to keep on curling the way they were in her heels. It'd been so long since she'd felt such overwhelming desire, and she was afraid that if she put the brakes on for a lengthy discussion about his sobriety, the spell would be broken.

And right now that wasn't an option, because there were life-altering kisses to be had.

Jess parted her lips, and her tongue snaked out, clueing him into the fact that she was right there with him. She wanted this. Wanted him.

When their tongues met, Sean hummed low in the back of his throat, and all of his quiet restraint slipped away. With a groan, he cupped the back of her neck, angled her face, and took the kiss deeper.

Jess had been kissed before, but no kiss in the history of all the world's kisses could ever compare to the sinful way Sean was kissing her at that moment. The longer it went on —one large, work-roughened hand cupping her nape, the other spread over her ribs at her side—the more turned on she became, her body growing warm and tingly in places she'd thought numb from disuse. And just when she thought she couldn't take it anymore—that she was going to self-immolate from the heat coursing through her—his lips slowed and then stopped.

He rested his forehead against hers, their breaths mingling in the small space between them. "I'm sorry. I should have asked first."

"No, you didn't need to."

He pulled back a fraction of an inch, and when their eyes met, his gaze was probing. "When I kissed you unsolicited before, you reminded me that I should have asked first."

"I did." She nodded. "But that was before I knew you. Before I knew how badly I wanted you."

Sean's lips hitched to the side in a sexy smirk. "You want me?"

Jess let out a small laugh and flicked her eyes down toward her chest and back up to indicate the nipples that had pebbled to tight little buds. Currently, they threatened to poke their way through the soft knit jersey that clung to her like a second skin. "These seem to confirm it."

Sean's tongue darted out of his mouth, and he licked a quick path over his bottom lip, his face ravenous as he ogled her curves. "Yeah, but it's good to get confirmation," he said. After a few more seconds lingering over her décolletage, he shook his head— as if to shake away his lustful stupor—and raised his eyes back up to hers. "For what it's worth, I'm trying to be a good man, Jess. A gentleman."

She set her palm to his cheek. "You *are* a good man. I wouldn't be here with you if I didn't believe that."

"Are you sure?" There was something she didn't quite recognize in his voice, a hesitation that seemed like he didn't know himself.

To assure him that she was one hundred percent on board with this plan, she did something completely out of character—something she'd heard other girls talk about but had never had the opportunity to experience for herself. Until now.

"Oh, I'm sure." With a grin, Jess bunched the fabric of her dress up around the tops of her thighs and tossed one toned, tan leg over his lap, straddling him in the front seat of his beloved Bessie Blue. Her grin stretched into a smile as she began plucking at the buttons of his dress shirt.

"I feel like a teenager again," he teased.

Jess fumbled with the second button from the top, and when it finally slipped through its hole, she raised her eyes to his. "I never did this as a teenager," she admitted, popping the next button and then the next until only one remained.

He stilled her hand. "Hey, look at me."

When she did, she expected to see pity there, but instead, all she saw was interest. And a challenging gleam in his eyes.

"I want this—I want *you*—but if you're at all unsure about getting it on in the front seat of my truck, we can stop right now. I have no problem moving this to a more traditional location. Like your couch. That was pretty comfortable." His eyes sparkled, and Jess knew he remembered the last time they'd spent time there.

While they'd started that evening baking pies, they'd finished it with Jess lying flat on her back, Sean resting atop her, as they'd kissed and rubbed against one another like horny teenagers. Eventually, his hands had ventured under her shirt, but he'd had enough restraint not to take things any further. It was likely the tamest evening he'd ever spent in a woman's arms, but for her, it had been the single hottest night of her life.

The fact that he was smiling so broadly now went a long way toward easing some of the uncertainty she'd felt about whether or not she might be too innocent for him. It wasn't like she was a virgin or anything, but Jess was pretty darn certain that if she wanted to hop on that whole born-again virginity train she'd once heard about, they'd welcome her with open arms.

But the thing about Sean, she was coming to realize, was that unlike other men she'd dated, he never made her feel wrong or foolish for who she was. In fact, he seemed to enjoy her all the more for it. Because at his core, he was a good, kind person. Flawed, sure, but they all were.

His words from earlier about trying to be a gentlemen came back to her. Well, as far as she was concerned, there was no *trying* about it. He simply was.

And she adored him all the more for it.

Jess tugged her hand free and unclasped the final button on his shirt as he watched her from hooded, lust-filled eyes. "I don't want to be anywhere else right now," she told him. "This, right here, is perfect." Before her new-found confidence could disappear, she parted the crisp white cotton of his dress shirt, leaned forward, and flicked her tongue out.

Sean hissed, and he gripped her thighs. She wasn't sure if that reaction was a good thing or a bad thing until he said, "Again," his voice low and husky.

Jess flicked her eyes up and watched for his reaction as

she licked a slow, meandering path over his nipple, so different from her own.

Sean's grip on her loosened, and then his hands slid up and around her waist where they came to rest at the small of her back. In the cleft between her thighs, she felt him grow impossibly hard.

As if by instinct—almost as if her body had a mind of its own, and it knew what to do even if Jess herself was uncertain—her hips rocked against the bulge in his dress slacks and they groaned at the same time.

One of Sean's hands slid up the length of her back to cup her neck and guide her to his lips, nothing at all hesitant about the way he kissed her now. He was a man consumed with passion for the woman in his arms, and as his pelvis rolled against her most intimate part and his tongue made love to her mouth, he told her without words how good she made him feel.

Meanwhile, Jess was using her words. *All the words*, it seemed. In fact, when their lips weren't tangled, she couldn't seem to keep her mouth shut. "Oh my god," was quickly followed by, "Please, more," which preceded, "You feel so good." And now, as Sean pushed aside the fabric of her dress to suck her lace-clad nipple into his wet, warm mouth, Jess kept repeating the same thing over and over and over again as she undulated over him, the crest of her passion rising higher and higher. "Yes, yes, yes."

"That's it, baby," he said, guiding her hips with one strong, sure hand as he pushed up against her, creating the most deliciously decadent friction. "Take what you need."

Jess screwed her eyes shut as a brief flash of embarrassment took hold. She was a twenty-six-year-old woman with very little sexual experience to speak of, riding her crush in the front seat of his truck in the middle of a vineyard. It was too ridiculous for words.

"Open your eyes, sweetheart. I want to see them when you make yourself come."

Jess's eyes fluttered open and their gazes locked as her orgasm barreled forth. One moment she was suspended, her body in a state of neither here nor there, and then all at once she fell, her passion crashing over her in exquisite waves that left her misty-eyed and breathless.

"Oh my," she whispered, as her body trembled. Sean brushed the hair back from her face, and his eyes flicked between hers for several long seconds. "You are one of the sexiest women I've ever laid eyes on," he said, gazing at her with wonder—as if he was as surprised by the realization as Jess was.

The truth was, she'd never been called sexy before. She'd quit the pageant circuit before she'd aged into the categories that required a lot of time parading in front of people wearing barely-there bikinis, so she didn't have much in the way of experience trying to vamp it up. Cute. Sweet. Shy. Naive. *Those* were words past boyfriends had used to describe her. Sean was the only man who'd ever looked at her like he wanted to eat her up with a spoon. Given how many times Jess had stared at a bowl of chocolate chip cookie dough ice cream, it was a look she knew well.

"No one's ever called me sexy before," she admitted, breaking eye contact to stare out the back window at the full, lush vines that gently swayed in the breeze in the golden glow of a harvest moon. Jess let her gaze linger for a moment on the tableau outside, memorizing the perfection of the moment so she could hold it close to her heart.

"You've gotta be kidding me. The moment I saw you jogging past the bakery that first morning, I couldn't believe my eyes. I'd never seen anything sexier than your curves glistening with sweat from your run."

She made a face. "Ugh, I don't know if I trust your idea of sexy. I was all sweaty and gross."

"I don't know about that," he said, his eyes gleaming. "Seems there are worse things I can imagine than working up a sweat with a beautiful woman."

Hmm, when he put it that way.

Suddenly, Jess was conscious of the fact that while she'd come, he hadn't. His bulge was pressed against her. A fact she wanted to rectify—immediately. And if she made him sweat while that happened, she'd concede that he was onto something with this whole glistening thing.

Jess swallowed her nervousness and gave herself a quick, inward pep talk. This was Sean, the man she was quickly falling for. The man who'd just let her get herself off on him. The man who hadn't pressed her to return the favor because he was a gentleman. If there was ever anyone she could say these words to, it was him.

"Do you have a condom?"

His eyes flashed with surprise—and perhaps a bit of wariness—before he nodded slowly. "I do."

"Want to help me work up a sweat now?" she asked playfully, her voice coming out on a squeak that wasn't the sexy vixen she'd been going for.

Sean cradled her cheeks in his big, warm palms. "Trust me when I say that I want nothing more than to work up a sweat with you, my sweet, sexy girl—" Jess's hope plummeted when she heard the "but" coming "—but when I do, I plan to take my time savoring every delectable inch of you. Unfortunately, the front seat of Bessie Blue isn't exactly conducive to the type of workout I'm imagining."

All at once that dashed hope sparked, rose, and went off like a firework. Or was that her ovaries?

"The first time I come with you," he continued, "is going to be in a bed, where I can fuck you properly." Sean's eyes were dark and molten as he continued whispering all the "proper" ways he planned to worship her.

And with each word that passed from his sexy, sinful lips, Jess knew that he was right. They needed a bed, they needed to be naked, and they needed all night long to turn those fantasies into reality. Alas, it was growing late, and Sean had to be at the bakery at four o'clock in the morning, while Jess had a run-through for her segment at the station that started at six. Tonight was not the night for long, leisurely lovemaking.

"What are you doing tomorrow?" she asked, her eyebrow raised high as she threw down the gauntlet.

Sean chuckled and claimed her lips in a quick, passionate kiss. "Spending the night at your place, it sounds like."

"Good, that's settled then."

"Mmm-hmm," he agreed, pulling her in for a kiss that somehow lasted another twenty minutes.

It was after midnight by the time she walked through her front door, kicking off her heels and stretching her arms high over her head.

And just like that, tomorrow had become today.

CHAPTER 13

Sean barely made it through his shift at the bakery the next morning. He came close to burning a batch of danishes when he thought about Jess's thighs closing around him. The points of Italian meringue on a cake he piped for a custom order reminded him far too much of her pebbling nipples. He was half hard all morning, staring at *baked goods*. Lord, he had a problem.

He had to slow down. He was trying to do the right thing. Jess wanted him, and he wanted her, desperately, but she had freely admitted that she was nervous. She deserved to be treated with respect. He had every intention of spending hours tonight making her come, on a bed, hot and sweaty and naked. But he could at least take her out to dinner first.

After he sold the last of the morning's almond croissants, he pulled out his phone.

Sean: Dinner at Frankie's tonight?

There was a long pause, and he glanced at his watch. Her TV segment was at seven. He'd meant to try to stream it on his phone, but he'd gotten caught up in shaping a batch of baguettes. Surely it was over by now. It was nearing ten.

Jess: Are you still coming over afterward?

He let a broad grin slide across his face.

Sean: I'm coming over. You'll be coming, too.

Her only response was the eggplant emoji, and his grin turned into outright laughter.

Sean: Pick you up at six.

Jess: See you then.

Sean: Um. Probably should warn you that I can almost guarantee my friends will all be there. If not right away, as soon as Max texts them.

Jess: As long as we're not taking them all back to my place with us, I think I can handle it.

She ended with a smiling emoji, and he sent one back and put his phone away, feeling the heat of anticipation wash over him again, tempered by an unexpected sense of ease. He was starting to call that soothing feeling the Jess Effect.

* * *

DINNER WENT EXACTLY as he expected it to, which was why he'd pre-apologized to Jess before they even left the car. When he ushered her in through the door, Max dropped a dish towel on the bar and dove for his phone. They'd been seated for all of five minutes when Noah and Angelica strolled through the door, looking effortlessly casual as though they'd meant to dine at Frankie's all along—even though his hair was still wet, and her socks didn't quite match.

Iain and Naomi didn't make it look nearly as good when they showed up two minutes later. The Irishman was breathing hard as though he'd been running, and the artist looked wildly around the room until she spotted Sean and Jess in the booth against the far wall. Sean rolled his eyes as the couple joined Noah and Angelica at the booth directly behind them. He leaned over the table toward Jess, who was still studying the menu.

"They're heeeeere," he sing-songed in a whisper.

He saw her lips quirk. "I know," she said quietly. "I saw them all come in. It wasn't subtle."

He chuckled. "Brace yourself."

When it came, the inquisition was quick. Noah leaned over the booth divider and pretended to be surprised to see them. "Sean, won't you introduce us to your friend?"

He sighed. "Noah Bradstone, meet Jessica Casillas-Moore."

"Bradstone?"

"Casillas?"

Noah and Jess spoke at the same time, both sounding surprised.

"Wait, are you one of Vincent's grandkids?" Noah asked. He glanced at Sean, a frown starting to gather on his face, like his opinion of Sean had somehow sunk further suddenly.

Jess nodded. "Are you Carter's son?"

"You know each other?" Sean asked.

Noah shook his head. "Not exactly. Her grandfather works with my dad. Knows more about grapes than anyone in the industry." He paused. "Although... you're the youngest?" Jess nodded, and he laughed. "I think I went to your eighth birthday party."

She smiled, but Sean could tell it was awkward. Not exactly the sort of thing you wanted to think about when you were on a date. He hadn't thought much about their age gap, but apparently Noah had been doing some mental math.

Angelica didn't bother to lean over the booth. She just came over and slid in next to Jess. "Hi. I'm Angelica."

Jess blinked. "Angelica Travis?" She turned her surprised

gaze back to Sean, and he winced. Sometimes he forgot Noah's fiancée was famous.

"It's so nice to meet you," Angelica was enthusing. "What do you do?"

"Um, I write a lifestyle and beauty blog, and I do some lifestyle segments on local TV."

Angelica's eyes lit up. "Lifestyle! My agent is always looking for new clients there! You should let me set you up!"

Before Jess could respond, Naomi leaned over. "I did your new logo last year, actually," she said mildly.

Jess blinked. "You're NK Designs?"

Naomi nodded. "I do most of my design work digitally. I didn't know it was you that Max—" she broke off and glanced over at the bar guiltily.

"Well, I love the logo," Jess said.

Iain pressed a kiss to Naomi's hair. "She does good work."

It all went downhill from there.

Max showed up, did some interrogating of his own, and then murmured something in Spanish to Jess.

Sean lost his patience.

"I lived in L.A. for ten years, you know. I might not be able to speak Spanish that well, but I can get the gist," he snapped at his friend. "And it's none of your business." He'd been able to translate enough to know that Max had asked Jess if she knew what she was getting into.

"Sorry," Max said, raising his hands in apology. "I forgot you were multilingual." He smirked, not looking particularly sorry.

Jess rolled her eyes at him. "I see why you're the single one," she said.

Sean beamed at her, while Max pretended to take an arrow to the heart. "Ouch," the chef said. "Maybe I should have asked you if *you* knew what you were doing, Sean."

"We're both adults," Jess said.

"Adults who would like to eat their tacos in peace," Sean added pointedly.

After that, they were mostly left alone, and Sean could only hope that his friends hadn't managed to kill any chance he had of naked time later.

When they left Frankie's less than an hour later, Jess's hand crept into his. And then on the drive back to her place, her fingers were busy on his thigh.

Apparently, his chances were still good.

* * *

THEY STUMBLED into Jess's bedroom attached at the lips, her fingers already working at his waist, slipping the button of his jeans open.

He set his hands at her hips, fingertips just under the edge of her shirt. "You sure about this?" he asked. "We can wait."

She took her hands off of him, and he felt the icy chill of disappointment until she shoved his hands aside and took off her shirt herself. "No waiting," she said, returning her lips to his.

He barely registered when his shirt came off, and his pants made it to the doorway when she threw them away. He was too occupied with her body, warm and smooth and the sexiest thing he'd ever touched. His hands shaped her breasts, still in their lacy confines, and he lowered his mouth to her nipple, relishing the soft gasp she made.

She pulled him backward until her thighs hit the bed, and then he took over, pushing her back with nothing but the pressure of his lips and tongue until she was lying full length on the bed, writhing and moaning his name.

"We've barely even started yet," he murmured against her velvet skin.

He slid her jeans down her legs and tossed them in the

general direction of his own, then hooked a finger in her underwear. "I like these," he said. "They match." Her bra and underwear were confections worthy of something he'd put on a cake, all delicate strands of white curling around her sweet skin in complicated patterns he wanted to lick until they disappeared.

She started to say something, then let it trail off into a moan as he dragged her underwear gently down, taking extra time to let his fingers slide along the sensitive skin of her inner thighs.

His lips traced the same path back up, and when his tongue slipped against her center, she nearly came off the bed. He paused. "Is this okay?"

"God, yes."

He grinned and went back to work. Jess was just as vocal now as she'd been in the truck, and he loved it. She wasn't shy about directing him to move to the left, or stay where he was, or go faster. He didn't always oblige—especially when she begged him to go faster. "Slower is better," he said.

"Says you," she gasped. "Oh!"

Then it was mostly vowels.

She came twice on his fingers and his tongue before he moved up her body. She twined her fingers bonelessly in his hair as he slid the condom out of its packet and rolled it on. His lips retraced her neck as he rocked gently against her entrance. He kissed her before opening his mouth to ask.

She beat him to it. "Yes, yes." She tilted her hips, and he slid forward. They both gasped and froze for a moment. He felt the blood drain from his head as her sweet heat enveloped him, inch by inch.

"Oh, god, Jess," he whispered.

She hummed with pleasure as he slid home, and he grunted as he fell deep into her. They rocked together slowly, then faster as she slid her foot up his leg. The change in angle flipped a switch inside of him, and he growled, grabbing her hips and completing the tilt of her body so that he was thrusting into her, against her. Her fingers closed around his arms convulsively, and she screamed his name as she tightened around him. The pressure pushed him over the edge he'd been teetering on, trying to extend the pleasure. He came hard, his body shaking against hers as he saw stars.

* * *

THE BUZZ of his phone woke him hours later. They'd been up together more than half the night, and he hoped the taste of her would never leave him. After the third time, they'd finally fallen asleep tangled together, and Jess was still sleeping, those dark lashes lying thick against her cheekbones. He raised a hand to trace her face, then thought better of it. She needed to sleep. She'd said she had another early call time this morning. He turned his head and used his free hand to pick up his phone. It was a text from Max.

Max: *You ready for what you're doing?*

Sean: *You're at least three hours too late to be asking that.*

Max: *I don't need sordid details, bro. You know what I mean.*

Sean: *You sound like Noah. When did you get so worried about my life?*

There was a pause, and then a different buzz indicated that Max had added Noah to the text, turning it into a group chat. Both of them kept the same odd hours Sean did for their respective jobs, so neither one thought anything of texting at four o'clock in the morning. Sean rolled his eyes.

Sean: *Seriously? Is this another intervention? Come on, guys.*

Noah: *Dude, we're proud of you for everything you've accomplished with your sobriety. We're just a little worried that it seems early to be bringing somebody else into all of this with you.*

Sean: *All of this?*

Max: She seems really into you. Did you tell her?

Sean: Not that it's any of your business, but yes, I did.

Noah: I know her grandfather, man. She's local. You can't just walk away if something goes wrong.

Sean stared at his phone for a long time before he answered.

Sean: You think I'm going to screw this up, don't you? Am I that bad of a guy?

Max: When you were drinking you were. We don't know if you've really changed.

Trust Max not to pull any punches. Sean let out a breath and closed his eyes, then breathed in slowly, trying to let the scent of Jess's hair soothe his frazzled nerves. Somehow the Jess Effect was struggling to overcome his friends' opinion of him. Hell, his own opinion, if he was honest. What the hell kind of dirtbag was he, anyway? He'd let his protégé die, he'd pickled himself in alcohol instead of trying to help in the aftermath, and now he was dragging Jess into the mess that was his life. His friends were right to be concerned.

He put the phone down without responding to the last text and started to ease his other arm out from under Jess and the pillow. It was time to go to work.

CHAPTER 14

After the fantastic, toe-curling night they'd just shared, the last thing Jess expected was the sound of her bedsprings startling her awake as Sean attempted to sneak out without so much as a goodbye. But that was precisely what was happening. She blinked her eyes all the way open as he shoved his legs into his jeans, cursing under his breath when his toe connected with the leg of her bedside table.

Jess pushed herself up into a sitting position and reached over to flick on the lamp at her side.

Sean's head quickly darted back around. "Sorry, I didn't mean to wake you."

"I kind of gathered that." She had about a million and one *other* things she wanted to say, but she didn't want to be *that* girl—the girl who cried at the first sight of rejection, the one who begged for an explanation, or the one who blamed herself for a man's bad behavior. Still, she had to know one thing. "Were you planning on saying goodbye?"

"I—" He huffed and blew out a long, slow breath, rubbing the heel of his palms against his eye sockets. When he pulled his hands away, his gaze connected with hers, and she saw the truth before he spoke the words. "I was going to let you sleep in."

Lie.

She pulled her feet up and crossed her legs, turning to face him. "I have to be up in an hour anyway, which you know."

He nodded once, and pulled his gaze away, scratching the back of his neck as he looked around the room—anywhere but at her.

Jess might not want to be that girl, but she was coming dangerously close to it. As it was, it took everything she had not to begin crying. His dismissal and apparent regret over their shared night together sliced like a hot knife through butter.

"Look, Sean. It's obvious you were going to sneak out, so go on ahead. I'm not going to stop you." She tossed the covers aside and stood up. Pulling a thin cotton robe off its hook, she wrapped it around herself, giving the bow an extra hard tug when she finished tying the knot. "You know where the front door is."

"I'm sorry, Jess. I really didn't mean for it to be like this." He pushed to his feet, his gaze averted.

"Yes, well. Be that as it may …" She pulled a deep breath into her lungs and swiped away tears that had begun pooling in her eyes.

Sean raised his head, his face a mask of regret. "I'm in a really weird place right now. I should have thought of that before … well, before all this—" he gestured between them "—but you were the first good thing that's happened to me in a while, and it was too hard to resist."

Jess rolled her lips between her teeth, biting down on them in the hope that the sting would override the one lancing her heart. She'd known deep down there was a chance rushing headlong into something with him when they hadn't hashed out his past could come back to bite her in the ass. She just hadn't thought it would happen so soon. In the end, their relationship—if that's what you could even call it—had amounted to three measly dates.

And now she had to say goodbye.

But first, "Just tell me one thing. Did this mean anything to you? Did *I* mean anything to you?"

Sean's eyes dropped to the floor, and he clasped the back of his neck in his palm. The same one, she couldn't help but remember, that had gently cradled her face as he'd entered her, their gazes locked on one another the entire time. Eventually, he raised his eyes back up and answered. "It did. More than you'll ever know."

"Then why? Was it something I said?" *So much for not sounding needy,* Jess's subconscious scolded, even as she continued. "Was it something I did—or didn't do?" She tried not to wince at that last question.

For having only slept with a couple of men in her life, and none of those past experiences what one could call 'out of this world,' Jess thought she'd held her own the night before. She'd also been pleasantly shocked to find that he seemed to bring out a wild, almost feral side of her that she hadn't known existed. Still, she wondered, had it been enough? Was he used to sleeping with women whose tastes ran more toward the type of kinks Jess had only ever read about in romance novels? Had she left him unsatisfied?

Sean took a few quick steps around the bed toward her, his hand outstretched. At the last moment, he halted and dropped his hand down to his thigh where his fingers beat a pulse against his jeans. He stared at her for a few long moments, his gaze assessing.

Jess could practically see the wheels turning in his head, presumably to come up with an answer that would let her down gently. Sean Amory might be a coward, but she didn't think he was needlessly cruel.

"Listen, Jess," he sighed, running his hand through his sleep-mussed hair. "I—"

She held up a hand to stop him. "It's okay; you don't need to explain. I get it. We had our fun, but now it's time to move on." Her voice trembled when she added, "I'm sorry I assumed this was something more. That's on me, not you."

He did step to her then, and when he pulled her into his arms and flush against his chest, she went willingly, all the fight gone out of her. She didn't know what it was about this man, but she was pretty sure there was nowhere else she'd rather be than in his arms. It didn't make any sense, but when he touched her, all felt right with the world—even as he seemed to make her world seem to fall apart around her.

"You didn't do anything wrong," he said, petting her hair with gentle sweeps of his palm before he dropped a kiss to the top of her head, his lips lingering. "You are amazing. Sweet, kind, and funny. Any guy would be lucky to have you. But at the risk of sounding like a tired cliché, it's not you—it's me. I'm all fucked up in the head right now, and I don't want to bring you down with me."

Ah, so that was it. Sean thought he was doing her a favor by walking away, never once stopping to consider that together they were stronger than the sum of their parts. Anger flickered in her chest, rising quickly past the sadness.

Jess pushed against his chest, and he loosened his hold on her. "Did it ever occur to you that I might want you to bring me down? Or better yet, I might be able to raise you up?" Her eyes flicked between his as she watched her words land and settle.

She knew she'd given him something to think about. She thought she'd gotten through to him until he took a step back, and then another, until more than a foot separated them. She wrapped her arms around herself, chilled by the sudden loss of contact, but also by the blank look that had come over his face. She knew she'd lost him.

"I know I have no right to ask, but can you give me some time?" It wasn't what she'd expected him to say. She'd expected a blanket no, a swift rejection.

Jess's heart thumped heavy in her chest. She wanted to say no, that if she weren't enough for him *now*, she wouldn't be enough for him later on either. And yet, deep down, she wanted him. More than she'd ever wanted any other man before in her life. She'd never felt like this about anyone, and she knew the likelihood of feeling it again for someone else anytime soon was slim to none. She didn't want to be in a relationship with a man who didn't appreciate her, but she also didn't want to give up on him either. Because, she thought, if she did give him time, he might come to realize that he felt the same way about her, too. He just had to do it on his own. And that might be worth waiting for.

She nodded once, not trusting her voice.

"Thank you," he mouthed, turning and leaving her standing alone in her bedroom at four-thirty in the morning.

* * *

JESS LOOPED her earring through the hole in her ear and took one last look at herself in the mirror above her dresser. She knew better than to leave her makeup to chance. Now, Jess did her own makeup before heading to the station. Thankfully, she was a pro at concealer, foundation, and eyeliner, so no one would ever know that she'd spent the last hour crying.

Jess opened her bedroom door and stopped in her tracks, the scent of coffee wafting toward her from the front of her house. Strange, she hadn't remembered programming her coffee maker the night before. Careful not to frown too deeply lest she ruin her makeup, she made her way into the kitchen where a fresh pot of joe was waiting for her, a plate of baked goods sitting next to it. Taped to the front of the coffee maker was a note, its contents scrawled in a heavy, angular slash that was a man's handwriting: *Sweets for the sweetest girl I know. Thank you for last night. For everything.*

Jess pulled the note from her coffee maker and stared at it for a few long seconds, her eyes intermittently darting to the blueberry muffin, apple fritter, and apricot danish on the plate next to it. Had Sean brought the sweets with him yesterday, expecting to spend a leisurely morning in her kitchen drinking coffee and eating pastry? Jess dropped her hand to her side and closed her eyes with a long sigh.

He was killing her. She said she'd give him time, and she'd meant it. But him leaving her little love notes as he departed her house like his ass was on fire wasn't fair to her. It sent mixed signals and made her feel even more confused than she already was.

With a heavy heart, Jess reached for the plate of pastries and stepped on the pedal of her trash can. Upending the plate, she watched as the tasty confections slid and tumbled their way into the garbage. When she stepped away, the lid shut with a clang, reverberating in the small, quiet space.

Even as he'd broken her heart, he'd offered her an olive branch, and Jess couldn't help but feel like she'd just tossed her chances with Sean into the garbage as well. Pastries! It was like he didn't know her at all.

Maybe that's because he doesn't, her subconscious inwardly sighed and Jess winced.

* * *

JESS CHECKED her rearview mirror to make sure the spot was

clear and merged into the other lane. The drive from her house to the station had given her time to think about everything that had happened earlier that morning, and while she was still upset at Sean's disappearing act, she had to admit that it was a good thing they were taking a step back. The pastries sitting in her garbage bin were a stark reminder that she had baggage too.

Baggage she still hadn't come clean about.

If it turned out that Sean worked through whatever it was that he needed to work through and decided he wanted to give them another shot, Jess knew she'd need to sit down and have a very real, very in-depth conversation with him. She wouldn't go so far as to say she had an eating disorder, but she knew her relationship with food wasn't healthy. That was something she needed to talk to someone *other* than Sean about. Someone not named Marisol, either.

As Jess pulled into a space at the station, her phone dinged from the center console where it was charging. Putting her beloved Honda in park, she picked it up to see who would be contacting her this early. Her phone typically didn't start harassing her until at least nine o'clock when the rest of the world came alive for the day.

Her lips pursed in confusion, Jess re-read the note on her screen.

(707) 123-4567: Hey Jess, this is Angelica. Angelica Travis. I don't know if you remember me, but I wanted to chat with you about something.

Jess chuckled. Angelica Travis, with her oversized personality and easygoing charm, wasn't someone you easily forgot. But what in the world could the retired-actress-turned-innkeeper have to discuss with her? Aside from Sean, they didn't have anything in common—at least not that Jess could discern. Angelica was tall and blonde and so comfortable in her own skin that it made Jess wince to think just how *un*confident she was. For a brief moment, she wished she could possess even an ounce of the other woman's seeming fearlessness. Then she might have been stronger in her showdown with Sean.

Curious, she typed back a quick response: *Hey there! Of course, I remember you. We met just yesterday, and you're not exactly forgettable. *wink* What's up?*

The little bubbles on her phone bounced, indicating that Angelica was responding. And when she did, Jess could hardly believe her eyes. *Meet her agent?* That was crazy talk. What could this Jai person want to discuss with a small-town beauty queen? She paused as her mind balked at that description. That wasn't *all* she was anymore. As Jess stared out her window at the TV station's logo, she allowed a flutter of excitement to unfurl in her belly—a stark contrast to the earlier flipping going on in her gut as Sean had told her they couldn't be together.

Speaking with a Hollywood agent might be bananas, and it might all be for naught, but suddenly, Jess couldn't wait to hear what the man might say. Something had to go her way, didn't it?

CHAPTER 15

You could have handled that better. Sean ignored the little voice in his head. He'd had to get out of there. He'd left her the pastries he'd brought with him the night before. In the heat of the night—God, what a night—he'd forgotten them, but he'd remembered at the last minute before he'd practically ran through the door on his way out. Leaving her baked goods wasn't much in the way of an apology, but it was all he'd had.

He worked the first few hours of his shift on autopilot, trying not to think about how good last night had been or how bad this morning had gone. Max and Noah were right— he wasn't ready to drag Jess down with him. It was selfish to want to be with her just because she made him feel good. Wasn't it?

Isn't that what love is for? He silenced the little voice again by firmly chopping apples and mixing batter for fritters. As he was portioning out the dough, the back door opened, and he looked up in surprise to find his mother reaching out for one of the spare aprons hanging on the wall.

"You're not scheduled this morning," he said.

She shrugged and put on the apron. He watched for a moment as she moved over to the racks where they stored supplies and began pulling ingredients out with practiced movements. Apparently, she didn't want to talk yet. Waiting was a two-person game. He identified the ingredients she was pulling down as the base for cinnamon rolls, the next item on his list, and reached over his head to pull down the appropriate bowl for her without comment. He handed it over and moved on to frying the fritters.

The quiet 'shuf' of flour falling into a bowl behind him lulled him, and he found himself easily falling into rhythm with his mom, edging sideways when she reached for something, handing her an ingredient as he finished with it, and performing the elegant dance of two people baking in one kitchen. It reminded him of when he was small, watching his parents in this very same place. They'd moved together so cleanly it had been hard to tell where one person ended and the other began. They'd baked together, assembling pastries with light touches while occasionally touching each other with similar gentle hands. He'd been tucked into a corner of the kitchen with a toy, or, sometimes, when he was a little older, he stood on a stool next to the counter to help with the mixing. His father had always let him punch down the yeast doughs.

But now his father was gone. The magic his parents had made in this kitchen was forever out of reach, and instead of the two of them here, in love, baking together, it was just him. How could the man who'd let Cal Grissom die fill those shoes?

He turned sharply to get his next ingredient and bumped into his mother's arm as she reached past him with a tray of shaped croissants headed for the ovens. The tray fell to the ground with a clatter, the croissants tumbling across the tiled floor and sticking to the grout, unrolling messily as they went.

"Shit. I'm sorry." He knelt to clean them up.

"It's all right," she said as she picked up the tray. "Accidents happen. I'll make some more."

"I'm sorry," he said again, not sure whether he was apologizing for bumping her, wasting the dough, or not being there all along to learn this dance.

He stuck close to his side of the kitchen while she remade the croissants. After she put them in the oven, she paused and watched him finish piping meringue onto lemon tartlets.

"You made some cookies and sold them," she said finally.

He finished the circle of little star-shaped dots around the edge of the last tartlet before he answered. "I did."

"Where did you get the recipe?"

"From the back of a spice bottle, if you can believe it." He turned to face her and saw her wince.

"Not using the family recipes is bad enough, Sean, but really? The back of a bottle? You might as well have slapped a Betty Crocker label on it."

"I'm pretty sure Betty doesn't make Mexican wedding cookies, Mom."

"Neither do we."

"The customers would beg to differ." He didn't know why he was arguing like this. The sensible thing to do would be to back down, apologize, and promise not to do it again.

"The customers? What would you know about the customers, Sean?" The hurt in her eyes made him bite back the angry response that came immediately to his lips.

"What do you mean?" he asked instead.

"You weren't here," she whispered. "All those years. How would you know what the customers want? And why should we trust you to find out?"

Sean's whole body went cold, then hot. "Is that what this is really about?"

She shrugged. He'd never seen his mother look uncertain about anything in his life. Watching her stare at him as though he were some unpredictable stranger who might walk away from her at any minute made him feel like his heart was cracking. He raised a hand to rub his chest, trying to ease the pain that wasn't really there. "Are you asking me what my plans are for the future?"

"Do you have some?" she parried. "If you want to stay, Sean, it would make me beyond happy. If you have ideas about the bakery, I'm happy to talk them over if it means you're thinking about your future here. Even if you don't—if you just want to work morning shift for the next twenty years and live in the apartment—I'm happy to have you here. But you have to be happy to be here, too. And I'm not sure you are. You never were before."

"People can change," he muttered.

"Have you?"

He didn't have an answer. "My shift is over," he said. "I see Paolo coming in. I'll see you later." He ran out of the bakery almost as fast as he'd run out of Jess's house that morning.

Oh, God, Jess. He didn't stop to think before he picked up his phone and called her.

"Sean?" She sounded suspicious and angry when she answered. He didn't care. The Jess Effect washed over him, and he took the first deep breath he'd managed since his mother had walked into the bakery.

"I'm so sorry," he said. "I was wrong."

"I know you were." She sounded as though she were talking to a child. "What made you figure it out?"

"I need you," he said simply. "Are you busy this weekend?"

* * *

SOMEHOW, by mutual silent agreement, they spent the entire weekend without talking about any of the issues that threatened to come between them. Sean picked her up on Friday evening, and they saw a movie, arguing amiably only about which romantic comedy to see, not whether to see one at all. They spent the night at her house, and for every time he made her scream his name, she managed to make his heart nearly stop as he breathed her in.

On Saturday, she made them both eggs for breakfast while he made a few phone calls.

"Got it," he said with satisfaction after he hung up. "Wow. These look amazing." How did she make even a plate of eggs look like they'd been cooked with extra attention and care? The Jess Effect, again.

"Got what?" She dug into her food, which she'd dressed with a spoonful of fresh pico de gallo.

"Kayaks." He reached out and stole a bite of her eggs, making sure to get a hefty portion of the tomatoes.

"Hey!"

"Mmm. Can I have some of that?"

She rolled her eyes. "It's in the fridge."

He rose and found the container in her fridge, right at the front. "You make this? I'd put it on everything if I had it sitting around."

"Even dessert?"

He laughed. "Maybe."

"I usually make it myself, but this week I stole some from my abuela because I was so busy."

He almost asked busy with what, but then he remembered that they weren't talking about anything except having fun. If he asked Jess about her week, he'd start talking about his, and he wasn't prepared to start thinking about the future beyond a couple of hours.

"I got us a couple of kayaks to take out later." He spooned the salsa onto his eggs and put the container away again.

She looked dubious. "Kayaks? Really?"

"You don't kayak?"

She waved her hand in a circle around her face and then downward toward her body. "Does this look like it kayaks?"

"You'll love it."

Four hours later, Jess whooped as her kayak slid through an opening between two rocks on the river. "You were right," she called over her shoulder as he followed her. "I do love this."

"Told you!" He navigated past the same obstacle and then caught up with her with a few wild paddle strokes. "My arms are getting tired. Want to stop?"

"No," she said with a grin. "But we can if you need to."

He pointed to a shallow area lined by gravel that was backed by waving grasses. "There are picnic tables up there."

"How do you know?" She angled her kayak toward the edge of the river, aiming for the gravel.

"Used to come here a lot in high school." He'd also come here after his dad's funeral and sat by the edge of the water and wept, but she didn't need to know that.

They grounded the kayaks, and he managed to get out of his without too much splashing. Jess had a leg on the ground when he reached her, but when he lifted her over the rest of the shallow water and swung her up onto the grass, she grinned at him. "Thanks."

He reached into his kayak's storage locker at the front tip of the boat and pulled out the wrapped package he'd tossed in when they'd started. "Lunch?"

She laughed. "You raided my fridge. I'm going to have to go shopping later."

He leaned forward to kiss her. "Guilty. Want to cook dinner together?"

She hummed low in her throat as he deepened the kiss, and their lunch went forgotten for several minutes.

After they ate, they wandered hand in hand around the little clearing, "Is that a path?" Jess pointed between the trees that lined the cove.

Sean squinted. "I think so."

She tugged him along behind her as she went to explore, and he followed, grinning at her enjoyment. Being outdoors with this woman was just as delightful as being indoors. They made their way down the path into the trees, and when they were out of sight of the river, Jess turned and pushed him against the nearest large trunk.

He grunted as his back hit the rough bark, but soon forgot everything but what her hands and lips were doing. Her mouth was on his chest, and then moving lower. Her fingers slipped into his jeans and slid along his length as he hardened. She gripped him and stroked in a gentle rhythm. He groaned and grabbed her waist, swinging her around to reverse their positions. He buried his face in her neck, licking every inch of her skin he could reach, and slid his hand into her shirt to shape her breasts. She wrapped her legs around him and rocked against his erection, and they both drew in a hard breath. Then he pressed her further against the tree and before he knew it his shirt was off, and her pants were halfway down. As her hand slid around him again and his body thrust helplessly against her he had a realization that made him want to slam his head against the tree.

"Fuck, Jess," he gasped. "I don't have a condom with me." What an *idiot* he was.

She gave him one last squeeze. "We should probably get home, then. Fast."

The tree was *nothing* compared to her bed.

Sunday was a repeat of Saturday, except instead of him

taking her kayaking, she took him hiking. And this time, he remembered to bring a condom along. They found themselves tucked into a crevice on a hidden trail, rocking against each other, his hands pressed against the boulders on either side of her head and her fingers scraping down his back as she gasped his name over and over again in rising tones. He slid one hand over her mouth to make sure nobody would hear them, and she bit his finger lightly and then stiffened against him, tightening as she came. He thrust up into her again and let her body take him to paradise.

Eventually, they grabbed an early dinner at a farm stand on the way back to town. He left her at her door with a kiss, savoring the last of the Jess Effect and wishing he could bottle it to get him through his shift the next morning.

"See you tomorrow for coffee after work?" she asked.

"It's a date." He didn't know how long they could sustain this relationship where they never actually talked about anything, but he drove away from her house feeling the most contented he'd ever felt in River Hill. That was worth something.

CHAPTER 16

"So that's the gist of it." Angelica's agent, Jai Carter, leaned back in his seat and linked his fingers over his flat abdomen, a satisfied grin splitting his lips. "What do you think?"

"I think it's a little much to take in," Jess answered honestly. "Doing segments on the local news is one thing, but my own show?"

"Nothing's set in stone—yet," he reminded her. "I still need you to fly down to L.A. to audition. But I have a good feeling about this." He raised his hands to tick off points in her favor on his fingers. "Unlike the other women auditioning, you know how to work a large audience and play to multiple cameras. And you're not intimidated by the professional side of this business. You've got the knowledge and the blog followers to back it up. It's one thing to know how to put on makeup; it's an entirely other thing to understand that this is a multi-billion dollar industry run mostly by suits with white, wrinkled skin."

Jai was right, of course. She'd been a part of the beauty industry in one form or another since she could walk. She had decades worth of experience standing in front of those old, wrinkled white men in expensive suits. The same one whose literal jobs were to judge her. She would *nail* this audition.

But that was only the first step on this grand adventure.

"I just want to clarify that if I get the job, I won't have to live in L.A."

Jai waved away her concern. "Not right away. The current plan is to tape three or four episodes in one day, and since this is an entirely new venture, there's no guarantee it's even going to take off. But the people who run RenoTV know a good idea when they see it, and they're willing to jump in with both feet with The Beauty Network. They'll work with you to make it work. But if this show takes off the way I think it will, this is only the first step in what I know is going to be an amazing career for you." He beamed at her, and his confidence was contagious: she believed him.

Which meant she heard the unspoken thought: she might not have to live in L.A. *now,* but she'd probably wind up moving there eventually.

It wasn't that she had anything against moving to Southern California, per se. It was just that she'd never really considered it before—mostly because everything she'd ever known and needed out of life was right here in the extended Bay Area. In fact, the longest she'd ever been away from her family was when she'd gone to Atlantic City to compete in the Junior Miss America competition and had then extended her trip to hang out in New York City for a few days afterward sightseeing and to shop for knock-offs in Chinatown.

And then there's Sean to think about, too, a tiny voice at the back of her head chimed in. Which was significantly more than Jess wanted to think about at the moment. Anytime she allowed her mind to drift to the handsome, confusing man, she became more and more confused about what was going on between them.

He'd said he wanted more time, only to turn around a couple of hours later and practically beg to see her again. He'd never explained his change of heart, and Jess hadn't pushed him to. The entire weekend they'd spent together, she kept telling herself to ask him why, but every time she worked up the courage to do so, it was as if he could sense the impending inquisition and would kiss her senseless instead. There was no other way to describe it: he kissed her, and she lost her damn mind.

The way he made her feel was unlike anything she'd ever experienced before, and even though they had problems, Jess didn't know if she was ready to give it all up—especially for a job she'd never considered as a viable career option. It wasn't like being a TV star had been her dream or anything. This was just a stroke of good luck, not the culmination of a life-long ambition. But there was that saying about gift horses.

One thing that *was* a life-long dream, however? To find the love of a good man and settle down and start a family. A real family, one that stayed together, like her grandparents. None of their children or grandchildren had managed it. It was a dream she'd never spoken aloud—never let herself want too hard or too much—but if she and Sean could iron out their issues, she honestly believed they stood a chance at true happiness. Maybe that was naive, given their start, but where this man was concerned, she was willing to believe in something other than the cold, hard facts. Because if she stopped to think about *those*, she might turn her back on him, and the chance for love.

But she was getting ahead of herself.

In the first place, there was no guarantee she'd be named the host of the show The Beauty Network was launching. And as Jai had just said, this was a very new venture. It could all go belly up tomorrow. And thirdly, Sean had to fall in love with her, too. And Jess knew they were a long way from *that* ever happening.

Bringing her thoughts back to the here and now, Jai pushed back from the table, his chair scraping across the tile of Angelica's kitchen floor. Jess stood to join him, and he reached across the table, his hand outstretched. "It was great meeting you in person, Jess. I hope this is the beginning of a long, profitable relationship." He winked, and she couldn't help the smile his remark brought forth.

"Likewise, Jai. I'll let you know when my flight is booked."

* * *

JESS STRETCHED out on her sofa, her phone at her ear. "Hey, you."

Sean had texted her a couple of minutes after she'd walked in her front door following her meeting with Jai, wanting to know if she had any plans that night. Instead of texting him back, she'd decided to call him to invite him over so she could share her good news about the audition in person. They'd been meeting for coffee the past few days at The Hollow Bean, but this was something she wanted to discuss in private. She could envision them sitting at her kitchen table, him pausing between bites of her vegetable lasagna to congratulate her and tell her how amazing she was. If he came around the table to kiss her and then carried her off to her bedroom for a round of celebratory sex, all the better.

"Hey," he answered, and Jess didn't think she was fooling herself when she heard the smile in his voice. "I missed you today."

"Oh really?" She twirled a lock of hair around her finger and then let it uncoil. "Tell me more."

"I was licking cinnamon sugar off my fingers at the end of my shift, and all I could think was that it wasn't as sweet as you."

Jess shivered, remembering the last time he'd licked *her* and feeling her insides tighten with anticipation. "Mmm," she breathed. "You don't taste so bad yourself."

And she wasn't just saying that either. Giving head had never been something she'd particularly enjoyed or excelled at, but the first time she'd taken Sean into her mouth, something had clicked into place, and she'd understood why some women loved giving blowjobs. She relished the way he felt on her tongue, his spicy scent filling her nose as she worked him over with her lips and tongue. He'd given her plenty of warning before he came, and while she could have finished him off with her hand, she'd wanted to drink his orgasm down the same way he'd done to her.

As if he could read her thoughts, he said, "Much as I enjoy thinking about making you come with my mouth and vice versa, we need to change the subject. I'm having dinner with my mom, and I don't want to walk into her kitchen sporting a raging boner."

Damn. She'd been looking forward to that celebratory sex too. Between her news and their flirty banter, she was all keyed up and ready to go. "Oh, well. I was going to invite you over to celebrate—naked, if you get my drift—but since you have other plans, I'll just have to rely on B.O.B."

"Bob?" he asked, his voice tight.

Jess sighed dreamily for added effect. "Until you, no one could make me come quite like B.O.B."

"For fuck's sake, Jess. I don't talk about—"

Immediately, her mood sobered. She'd thought they were teasing, but it was apparent he didn't get the joke. "Hey. I'm just teasing. I wouldn't—"

"Teasing me about some other dude—"

This was just out of control now. "Sean, B.O.B. is my vibrator," she interrupted before he could fling some unfounded accusation her way. "You know, a Battery Operated Boyfriend?"

A few beats passed in silence while she listened to him breathe on the other end of the line. And then he chuckled. "Christ, I walked right into that one, didn't I?"

She chewed on her lip with mingled annoyance and worry. "I'm sorry. I didn't mean to upset you."

"I'm not upset."

"But you were." It wasn't a question. The restrained fury in his voice had come through the line loud and clear. They might be keeping secrets from one other, but she needed him to understand that even though she didn't know *everything* about him—about what was going on in that complicated head of his —she *knew* him. He'd been upset by the idea of her having been with anyone but him. It was an antiquated, sexist notion that alternately made her bristle with indignation and warm with delight. She'd never had a man get jealous before. It wasn't something she wanted to encourage, but a small part of her preened with satisfaction that someone as handsome as Sean Amory might feel something close to anger at the idea of shy, quiet Jessica Casillas-Moore being a little bit of a sex kitten.

"Okay, I was."

There it was again, that tiny spark of delight.

"Trust me, Sean. You have nothing to be jealous about. I wasn't lying when I told you—"

"I know, Jess. I just … never mind."

"No, tell me." Jess sat up and pulled a blanket over her lap. So many of their conversations were light, frivolous things. She yearned for him to open up to her, to share his thoughts and feelings—even if they were about something as unwelcome as their previous lovers. "You just what?"

He sighed, and she could picture him running his hand through his hair, a tic she was coming to learn signaled when he felt overwhelmed or uncomfortable. "I sometimes wonder why you haven't told me to go fuck myself already. You had the perfect chance to on Friday, but you welcomed me back into your life with open arms and a warm smile. Any guy would be lucky to have you, but for some reason, you're wasting your time with me."

Her heart broke for him. Someday, she'd find out why he seemed to hate himself so much. Something had broken Sean Amory, and while Jess didn't think she could fix him long term, she hoped her love would act as the glue that would bind the fragmented pieces of his heart and soul back together in those moments when he felt like breaking apart all over again.

"Don't you think it's up to me to decide who's worth my time?" she asked, her tone gentle. She didn't care how many times or how many ways she had to say it, some way, somehow, she'd prove to him that she was strong enough to weather the storm. Not *for* him, but rather, *with* him.

"Yeah," he agreed, while not really agreeing.

She got the impression he was placating her, and that made her angry. If they were going to work, he had to let her in. He had to *hear* her and believe her when she said she wanted to stand by his side.

But that wasn't a conversation to have on the phone.

"What are you doing this weekend?"

He sighed, a world-weary sound if ever there were one. "I hadn't thought about it."

Which meant he hadn't thought about spending it with her. No matter; she'd *make* him think about it, even if she had to drag him kicking and screaming. She recounted her conversation with Jai, her voice becoming more and more animated the longer she went on. "So I have to fly down to L.A. on Friday morning for the audition. Come with me."

Jess waited for his reply. And waited. And then waited some more.

"Sean?"

He swallowed deeply, the sound of his throat bobbing reaching her ears. "Yeah, that's not going to happen." His voice cracked on the last word.

Pain lanced at her heart at the intensity of his response. He was shutting her out again. Shutting down.

To hell with that.

"Why?" she demanded, her anger rising. She'd been so understanding, so … nice. It was time to call forth a bit of that Casillas fire her siblings were best known for. Jess was tired of being accommodating, of putting other people's wants and needs before her own. Of trying to always be *liked*. She cared about Sean, but she deserved better than the hot and cold he kept giving her. She deserved an explanation, and she was damn sure going to get one.

"I don't want to talk about it."

"Tough," she shot back as she rose to her feet. Pacing the length of her living room, she continued, "If I'm good enough to fuck seven ways to Sunday, I'm good enough to be told why you keep shutting me out."

"It's not you, Jess. It's me."

She snorted. "Yeah, try again, Sean. I may have bought that the first time, but not again."

"I just can't go to L.A. Okay?"

Jess breathed deeply and let it out in one long, slow gust. "No, it's not okay." And then she hung up on him.

CHAPTER 17

Sean stared at the phone. It was shaking. No, that was his hand. She'd asked him to go to L.A. She'd asked him, and he'd said no, and then she'd hung up on him.

No, that wasn't how it had gone. Sean shook his head. He wasn't being fair to Jess. *What else is new?* She had no idea why he couldn't go to L.A. He still hadn't told her anything about his past. He could tell she'd been so excited about this new opportunity—and when had Angelica hooked Jess up with her agent, anyway?—and he'd been unsupportive, to say the least. He scrubbed his hand over his face. Should he call her back? Apologize? Explain?

The problem was, he wasn't sure he had the capacity to sit there and describe what had happened, explain what he'd done and not done, how he'd failed his protégé. He tried to picture himself going to L.A. with her, stepping off the plane into the familiar airport, driving through the streets he'd driven a thousand times before. He felt the stirrings of nausea rise in his throat. He leaned his head against the steering wheel and banged it softly against the hard surface. *Get it together, Amory.*

A gentle tapping on the truck's window made him lift his head. His mother stood in the driveway, watching him with an inquiring expression. He sighed and opened the door.

"Want to talk about it?" she asked as he got out.

I don't want to talk about it. His earlier comment to Jess came back to him, and he scowled. "No."

Her eyebrows went up. "I see."

Shit. He hadn't meant to snap at her. "Sorry."

Sean followed his mom into the house, where they sat down to dinner and managed to talk about nothing of substance for the next two hours. Apparently, she was back to waiting him out. Twice, he was on the verge of opening his mouth to tell her that Jess had invited him to L.A. and ask how he should be feeling. That's when he'd remember he hadn't told her about Jess at all, and the idea of explaining everything on top of revealing the heavy weight of terror that seemed to settle over him every time he considered stepping off the plane in Los Angeles was just … too much.

Too much to blurt out over dinner, even over his mother's pork tenderloin with roasted apples. She'd made it especially for him, he knew. And guilt gnawed at him that he wasn't appreciative enough, grateful enough. She'd always been here for him, no matter what. And he couldn't even bring himself to tell her that he had a girlfriend.

Of course, he might not have that anymore, either. Jess had been pretty angry. Rightfully so. Before he lost his girlfriend and mother in one fell swoop, he made a concerted effort. "This is delicious. Thanks for inviting me."

His mother smiled. "I'm glad you like it."

He managed a smile in return. "You know I like it. It's been my favorite since I was ten."

"Why mess with a sure thing?"

Why, indeed. He'd done nothing but mess with sure things lately. "Maybe you can teach me to make it sometime."

He'd caught her by surprise, and he wished he could relish the moment. "You've never asked to learn anything but baking."

He shrugged. "I've been thinking I ought to know how to do more than heat up leftovers." He summoned his best impression of his smooth-charmer smile for her.

"I taught you more than that in high school," she pointed out.

"Sure, but not the good stuff." He waved a forkful of pork at her. "Why were you holding out on me?"

Her rich laughter filled the air, and he relaxed a little bit. "Holding out! Sean Amory, it was like pulling teeth to get you to do anything in the kitchen that wasn't baking."

"See, now I'm older and wiser, and I realize that a man can't live on scones alone."

"Why the sudden interest in cooking real food?"

"Hunger?" he improvised.

"Nice try." She narrowed her eyes. "I'll assume it's either a girl or a tapeworm."

"Definitely tapeworm," he teased.

She chuckled. "I'll teach you and your tapeworm any recipes you want."

"Are any of them in the cookbooks?" He nodded his head toward the other room, where the precious Amory Recipes resided.

She shook her head. "All baking, all the time, your ancestors." She paused. "There might be a couple of recipes for savory tartlets and quiches, but that's about it."

"I love quiche."

"We can make one together on your next day off if you'd like. Maybe you can take it somewhere to impress your … tapeworm."

He narrowed his eyes at her, but she just grinned at him.

Later, back in his apartment, he slumped down into the

old, lumpy office chair at his desk with a sigh and flipped open his laptop. Checking email was the only activity he had left in him at this point. He'd spent the entire evening pretending like nothing was wrong, and now he was exhausted.

He clicked through sale notifications from stores he hadn't shopped at in years, spam emails about everything from class reunions to penis enlargers and found his cursor hovering over the last unopened email in his inbox.

From: gil@unitedmedia.net
To: sean.amory@gmail.com
Subj: Your Appearance on 'Died Too Soon'

Hello, Mr. Amory,

My name is Gil Cartwright, and I'm a producer with United Media. Among other projects, we produce a series you may have seen on either HistoryNet or the Music Channel called 'Died Too Soon.' This documentary-style series comprises hour-long episodes featuring an in-depth exploration of a celebrity who passed away at an early age. We're beginning production next Friday on our episode about the time period surrounding Cal Grissom's death, and as one of his close friends and colleagues, we'd be grateful for you to appear and consent to an on-camera interview to tell your story.

Please let me know if you'd be interested; I'm very excited to meet you. Let me know how I can help in any way to make this happen. Our fans are eager to see Mr. Grissom's story told, and I know you're one of the best people to tell it. We have agreements already in place from several other members of his former team, as well as family members, but you're the key piece of the puzzle! Looking forward to speaking with you.

Sean slammed his laptop shut, breathing hard. They were filming? Had others agreed to be interviewed? They wanted him to tell his story? What story? That he'd failed Cal, failed Jess, failed his mom? Failed every person who'd ever really mattered to him?

He buried his head in his hands.

He wished he could call Jess and let the comfort of her existence wash over him. But she was done letting him use her. He'd been a jerk, and he'd been thinking only of himself and how she made him feel better. The second she'd invited him into her life, he'd leaped away like a startled deer. No wonder she'd hung up on him.

He opened the laptop again, minimizing the open window as quickly as he could so he wouldn't have to see the email. He opened a new browser window and pulled up YouTube. With shaking fingers, he typed 'Cal Grissom' into the search bar and hit enter. When the page loaded, he clicked the video at the top of the list—the one that had first gotten the kid his recording contract. Cal had had millions of followers, kids who'd adored him for his smooth voice and infectious smile. The floppy-haired good looks hadn't hurt him, either.

Sean clicked play and let the music wash over him. When the video ended, he moved on to the next one, then the next, watching every video available, from the first one Cal had released as an awkward fourteen-year-old to the last, the song Sean had produced. It had gotten him a framed platinum record. He'd tossed it into a box after Cal had died and hadn't looked at it since. The memories were harder to hide, though.

He set the videos to replay and left the music playing in the background as he opened a new tab and googled 'Died Too Soon.'

He read through the search results, huffing with annoyed

laughter at fan sites devoted to conspiracy theories about murder cults, and raising an eyebrow at the thinkpiece that said that the show treated celebrities like science experiments. A large number of comments contained enthusiastic praise for the show. It had been conceived by a former news journalist and a documentary producer who both had wives who loved celebrity gossip. They'd started with Heath Ledger, moved on to Prince, and worked their way through the entire '27 Club'—musicians like Amy Winehouse, Kurt Cobain, and Jim Morrison who'd died at twenty-seven years old. The show had a rabid following who enjoyed its thorough and sensitive approach to beloved celebrities and the sometimes unfortunate circumstances of their deaths.

He noted with no small amount of surprise that several episodes featured interviews with friends and family members of dead celebs who hadn't been willing to appear or be quoted elsewhere. One of them had even given a quote to an industry magazine that said appearing on the show had been "like therapy."

He snorted. That was coming on a little strong. Not that he had much room to talk. He was a mess. Would sitting on a stool with cameras in his face talking about the worst day of his life really help? He couldn't imagine it.

Maybe it would help to journal, though. That was the sort of thing therapists told you to do, right? He opened the deep drawer on his right, hunting for pen and paper. He pulled out a pair of boxers (*why, drunk Sean?*) and one of his mom's prized Amory recipe books and kept digging until his hand closed around something glass.

He froze.

The familiar shape of a bottle slid along his fingertips, and he breathed in low and slow as he drew it out. Whitman's Special Blend. Iain and Maeve had given him a bottle of their whiskey when the distillery first opened. He must have missed it when he'd cleaned out the rest of the alcohol in the apartment.

He stared at the bottle, the amber liquid glinting in the warm light from his desk lamp. The old itch began to grow under his tongue, accompanied by an ache of longing for oblivion. What if he just had a quick drink before he looked at the email again? It would be so much less painful to take the edge off. Just an edge. It wasn't like he was going down to The Hut to get blitzed.

He set the bottle down on the desk next to his computer and stared at it until the liquid settled, the vibrations from being moved around fading into stillness. He was still, too. His eyes couldn't seem to look away. His hand rose toward it but brushed against something else on the desk on its way up. The cookbook. An Amory oldie. He looked at it, a memory niggling at the corners of his mind. He'd been searching for something in it, he remembered. A whiskey glaze, for the apple fritters. To make changes to the bakery. If he stayed. His eyes strayed to the bottle again, and he sat back in his chair, staring at the two objects, his hooded gaze flickering back and forth. Bottle and cookbook. Cookbook and bottle.

Cookbook *or* bottle.

Finally, he made a decision. And acted on it.

CHAPTER 18

"**W**ait a minute. You're doing what?" Marisol leaned forward, slapping her palms down onto their grandparents' kitchen table.

"I'm auditioning for a TV show on Friday." Jess lifted her chin. She refused to be cowed by her sister's patent incredulity.

"I heard you the first time," Marisol shot back. "I just didn't believe you. You can't act."

Jess wanted to argue, but Marisol wasn't wrong. She'd once attended an improv class with a group of friends and had been so bad the instructor had asked her not to come back. "It's not for a *role*. I'd be hosting a show focused on beauty and wellness."

"Why you?" Manny sailed into the room and toward the fridge, where he pulled out a can of beer and chugged down half of it in one long swallow.

Jess rolled her eyes. "You may not have noticed, but those *are* my areas of expertise."

"Because you're a former beauty queen? I used to play football, but no one is calling me to coach the 49ers."

"That's because you rode the bench." Robert dropped into the seat next to Marisol and popped a guacamole-topped chip into his mouth. "At least Jess has trophies, sashes, and crowns."

"At least *I* made the team," Manny replied, joining his siblings at the table. "You were a nerd."

For the next ten minutes, her siblings traded insults about their perceived shortcomings while Jess sat there silently wondering why she even bothered. She didn't ask for much from her family; just that they support her when good things happened. Or maybe that they at least remembered that she had a career. It wasn't being a beauty queen that had paid her bills or bought her house; the income from her writing and TV segments had. TV segments that had landed her this current opportunity.

And despite Sean's reaction when she'd invited him to tag along with her to L.A., this audition was a *very* good thing. Especially now that their relationship had crashed and burned. Getting out of River Hill was looking more and more like her best option. She didn't want to count her chickens before they hatched, but if the audition went well, she'd talk with Jai about getting a small place near the studio. Given the fires last year, she'd have no trouble finding someone to rent her house in River Hill. Housing in Sonoma was at a premium.

"Tell me more about this audition, mija." Her grandma sat down in the empty chair next to her, their knees angled toward one another.

Jess leaned closer, so they could better hear one another over the noise of her squabbling siblings. "You know Angelica Travis?"

"The actress with that hotel show?"

Jess nodded. "I met her through a mutual friend, and the

next thing I knew, her agent called to discuss a new show that he thinks I'm perfect for."

"That's fantastic. Who's going with you to Los Angeles?"

"You're going to L.A.?"

Jess turned to face Manny. All three siblings were staring at her expectantly. "Yes. That's what I've been trying to tell you."

Robert crossed his arms and glared at her. "I don't like it."

Jess's temper flared. "It's a good thing I didn't ask you, then, isn't it?"

As if she hadn't said a word, Manny set down his drink and turned to their sister. "You need to go with her."

Marisol huffed. "I can't just drop everything to go traipsing off to Hollywood with this one."

"Well, *someone* needs to go with her."

She looked to her grandmother for support, but the older woman simply shrugged as though she agreed that Jess needed supervision. Wordlessly, Jess stood and exited the room, the sound of her siblings' bickering fading as the door swung shut behind her. It took them a few minutes to realize that she'd left, and when they did, they stormed into the den to accuse her of not taking them seriously.

"You think?" Jess glared at Robert. "I can't imagine why not."

"Be reasonable, Jess."

She pointed angrily at her sister. "No, *you* be reasonable, Marisol. I own my own home, and I run a successful business. I don't need a fucking chaperone!"

Manny took a step back and raised his hands. "Whoa. What's your problem?"

"*You're* my problem," Jess shot back, looking pointedly at each of them. "You treat me like a baby."

"You *are* the baby," Robert said, and Jess turned on him.

"No," she said through gritted teeth. "I am the *youngest.* That doesn't make me a baby."

"Okay, fine. You're not a baby. Happy?"

Jess shook her head. "Nothing about this makes me happy."

"If you had a boyfriend, this wouldn't be a problem."

Jess's jaw dropped. *"Excuse* me?"

"If you had a boyfriend who could look out for you— someone who would make sure you aren't being taken advantage of—we wouldn't be worried so much."

"I do have a—" Jess realized what she was about to reveal and shut her mouth. She hadn't told her family about Sean because she hadn't wanted to endure their version of the Spanish Inquisition. Now, there was nothing to tell after all. "I don't need a man to take care of me. This isn't the fifties."

"Go back to the first part," Marisol said, crossing her arms. "Spill the beans."

Jess shook her head, and her eyes darted to the door. They were all waiting for Vincent Casillas to get home from the vineyard before they sat down to dinner, but Jess wasn't sure she wanted to stick it out. If she pushed it, she could reach the door in four quick strides and be to her car before anyone could catch her. There were some benefits to being the smallest and fastest Casillas grandchild. "It's nothing. Forget I said anything." She shifted a few feet to the left, preparing to execute her getaway plan.

Robert's eyes narrowed as he watched her, and he settled lower into something that looked alarmingly like a catcher's stance before looking over at Marisol. "You going to do something about this?"

Marisol lifted her shoulder and huffed—again. It seemed all she did these days was huff about things Jess said or did. Frankly, Jess was tired of it. She was tired of *all* of her siblings. She loved them dearly, but she wasn't sure she liked them all that much. She was sick of the way they treated her —like she was some sort of estupido who couldn't function in the world. Well, screw that. This ended today.

They were still bickering about what to do with her. She brought her fingers to her lips and let loose a whistle that immediately put a stop to the conversation. All at once, three heads turned her way.

"Damn, Jess. What was that for?"

She planted her hands on her hips and glared at Manny, Robert, and Marisol in succession. "Who I date is none of your business. Besides, Sean and I aren't together anymore."

"Is this the guy you started to tell me about at the coffee shop?" Marisol asked.

Honestly, Jess could barely remember that conversation. She'd been so distracted remembering her and Sean's first kiss that most of what Marisol had said had flown in one ear and right out the other. Dimly, she recalled blurting out that she was seeing someone when her sister had tried to set her up with some random guy she knew through the boys' school. "Yes."

"What's his name?" Manny interjected.

All the fight suddenly went out of Jess. "It doesn't matter. We're done."

"He hurt you," her other brother observed.

"No," Jess said. "I mean, yes. But like I said, it doesn't matter. I'm moving on."

"What's. His. Name?" Manny's voice was less curious now and much more menacing.

Jess blew out a long sigh. She didn't want to discuss her relationship with Sean with her brothers and sister, but she knew if she didn't give them something, they'd never let up. "Sean. It's Sean, okay? Are we done here?"

"Sean who?"

Jess turned to Robert. "I doubt you know him. He lives

in town. His family's some kind of big deal. Founding family, or something. You're not going to be running into him."

Manny's head fell back, and he pinched the bridge of his nose, muttering something about "give me strength" in Spanish. "Amory. She was dating Sean Amory," he said, turning to Robert.

"You were dating Sean *Amory?*" Marisol screeched. Her brothers whispered darkly between themselves.

Jess scowled at her siblings' reaction. So they couldn't believe someone like *her* would be able to land someone like *Sean?* Yes, he was handsome as sin, and she assumed his family was rich, but why *wouldn't* they think she was good enough for him? She was beautiful too, and she wasn't overly flattering herself to think so. She had the sashes and trophies to back it up. She'd been a damn beauty queen, after all. And she was sweet, caring, and loyal. She was a catch! It stung that her family didn't think the same.

"Thanks for the vote of confidence, guys, but if that's everything you've got, I think I'm going to head home. I wasn't really in a great mood when I got here, and you all have only made it worse."

She tried to push past her brothers, but Manny stopped her. "Not so fast, little sis." With his hand wrapped around her bicep, he dragged her to the old, worn sofa and pushed her down into it. "Start talking."

Jess flicked her eyes between her brothers who stood sentry in front of her, their arms crossed over their chests and identical scowls marring their handsome faces. On the other side of the room, Marisol blocked the door, preventing Jess from exiting even if she were able to get past these two. Apparently, this was a team effort. With a resigned sigh, she leaned back against the sofa cushion. She was clearly going to be there a while, so she might as well get comfortable. "We were only dating for a couple of weeks. It wasn't anything serious."

Lie! her inner voice spat. *You are a lying liar who lies.*

Except she wasn't lying. While Jess might have thought things were moving in that direction, it was clear now that Sean hadn't felt the same. It took two to tango, and Jess had been dancing alone.

"How could you go out with someone like that?" Manny flung out his hands. "I mean, come *on*, Jess. And you wonder why we don't trust you to make good decisions for yourself."

Marisol shook her head solemnly. "So naive."

Jess's head bounced between her siblings, and she frowned in confusion. There was being overprotective, and then there was this—whatever it was. Their response didn't make any sense. Sure, Sean had admitted to having had a drinking problem, but from the way Manny, Robert, and Marisol were behaving, you would think he'd killed someone.

"How could *you* go out with someone like *him?*" Manny repeated.

Jess rolled her eyes. "You mean someone handsome, kind, and caring?" While she might be hurt at the way Sean had so callously brushed her aside, she couldn't deny that when he wasn't a confusing asshole, he'd been one of the nicest men Jess had ever met. Deep down, she believed that was who he really was. The asshole part was temporary. Hopefully.

Robert snorted. "He's not kind, Jess. That's how guys are when they want to get in your pants."

"You don't know him," she fired back reflexively, trying desperately to ignore the small part of her brain that silently agreed with him. If the seed of doubt was planted, she knew it could sprout into a thick, ugly weed if she let it.

Manny shook his head. "We do know him. We went to school together. He was every bad cliché you've ever heard about: captain of the football team, dated the head cheerleader, was named prom king."

Jess raised her chin defiantly. "So what? That's a crime now? Sounds to me like you're just jealous."

He muttered something under his breath, and Robert took up the reins of the conversation. "We're not jealous. He's a dick, Jess. Always has been, always will be. And he's dangerous."

"You don't know him."

Marisol threw up her hands and marched over to join them. "Try as you might, you're not like him, Jess. *We're* not like him. He's one of *them*, and we're one of *us*. Why is that so hard to understand?"

Jess shot to her feet. "Probably because you're talking in riddles. Them. Us. This isn't some girl-from-the-wrong-side-of-the-tracks romance novel, and he's not some evil villain in one of the boys' superhero movies."

Marisol sighed and shook her head while Manny took hold of Jess's hand. "Are you sure about that?" he asked quietly. "How much do you *actually* know about him, Jess?"

The matching looks on her sibling's faces stopped Jess's response from spilling forth. All three of them bore solemn expressions of sheer horror backed by pity. For her. She wanted to defend Sean against their insults and innuendo, but sirens were blaring in her subconscious. Clearly, they knew something she didn't. "What aren't you telling me?"

"She doesn't know," Manny said to Robert who looked to Marisol, his eyebrows raised and his eyes wide.

"I don't know what?"

"Obviously she doesn't know," Marisol sniped, stepping between them to stand next to Jess.

"Jess ..." Manny cleared his throat and started again. "Jess, he *killed* someone."

Her body fought against her brother's words. Her breath

hitched, and her heart lurched. Adrenaline coursed through her veins, and her ears rang as tiny pinpricks of light danced in front of her eyes. "No," she whispered, her knees feeling weak. "That's not true."

Robert nodded. "You remember that singer, Cal Grissom? Sean Amory was his agent or producer. I'm not sure which. All I know is Sean's the one who threw the party where Cal overdosed. Rumor has it he's the one who supplied Cal's drugs."

"No." She shook her head wildly. None of this made any sense. Sean had a drinking problem, not a drug problem.

Are you sure about that? her subconscious queried.

She was sure, wasn't she?

Her mind reviewed the few conversations they'd had about his past. When they'd talked about his position at the bakery, he'd told her things had fallen apart down in Southern California, but he'd never told her in what way. Instead, the conversation had focused on the here and now, and the difficulties he faced with his mother and her expectations for the bakery. She'd known he'd worked in Hollywood in some fashion—that had been one of the reasons she'd wanted him to join her on her trip down there next week—but he'd never offered up any specifics about his actual job.

The problem was, Jess hadn't probed, either. That wasn't what their relationship had been about. They were getting to know one another without all the baggage associated with their unhappy pasts. And she'd been guilty of holding things back, too. Because she didn't want Sean to dig too deeply into her issues with food, she'd chosen not to dig either. And now she was sinking in a pile of quicksand of her own making.

"No," she whispered again as her sister eased her back down onto the sofa.

"How did you not know?" Marisol asked gently.

"I never asked," she admitted.

"Why didn't you Google him?"

"I don't do that," she answered sadly. "Someone did it to me once, and the date was awful. I spent an hour answering questions about things they'd read online."

Marisol shook her head. "You poor, naive girl."

For once, Jess didn't feel the need to defend herself. Perhaps Marisol, Manny, and Robert were right—she wasn't as capable as she thought.

CHAPTER 19

Jess didn't answer her phone the first time Sean called. He'd really fucked up. He left her a message, but he didn't know how coherent it was, so he called her again. This time, she picked up just as he thought it was going to jump to voicemail again. There was silence on the other end of the line, and then her voice, strange and distant in a way that baffled and horrified him.

"What do you want, Sean?"

"I want to apologize."

"Is that all?"

"I—"

"Apology accepted. Have a good life."

"Wait! Jess, wait!" His heart was beating like he'd just run a marathon.

"What?"

"Can we please talk? I have some things I really, really need to tell you. And ask you."

She didn't answer, but he could hear her breathing. He pictured her at home, curled up on her comfortable couch, bare feet tucked under a throw blanket. "Jess?"

"You can come over."

"I'll be there in ten."

He made it in eight, driving Bessie Blue down the quiet streets of River Hill like they were fenced off and striped out for an Indy car race. Her front door was ajar, indicating he should make his way inside. He found her exactly how he'd pictured her, except her face was smooth and expressionless, not the warm, laughing Jess of his imagination.

"Hi," he said awkwardly.

"Hi." She didn't offer him a drink or invite him to sit down. She didn't do anything but stare at him patiently.

He sank onto the opposite end of the couch, dropping his keys onto the end table with a clatter. He watched as the weight of his body on the cushions threw her off center. He tried not to think of it as a metaphor.

"I'm sorry about the way I acted on the phone the other day," he said.

"You should be," she said evenly. "You were a jerk."

He sighed. "I *am* a jerk, present tense."

She raised an eyebrow, and he got the sense that she wasn't surprised.

"I haven't been totally honest with you about everything that's been going on with me. It isn't fair to you."

"Why don't you start now?"

He took a deep breath. "I want to. It's hard, though."

"Life is hard," she said.

He winced. The Jess Effect was absent today. His fault.

"When I was in L.A., I was a record producer." She nodded, so he went on. "I had a client, tons of talent. Young kid."

"Cal Grissom," she said flatly.

"You know?"

"My brothers told me that you killed him."

"I did."

Her eyes widened. It wasn't what she'd expected to hear, he thought. It wasn't entirely what he'd expected to say, to be honest. Time to tell her all of it then, so she could run screaming from him like she should have in the first place.

"I recruited him to the label. Flew him out to Hollywood, took him to parties, introduced him to my idiot friends. Trying to lure him into signing with us by bribing him with all the usual suspects."

"Drugs?" Her voice was hard.

Sean shook his head. "I've never done them, but I can't say they weren't around. I thought I could keep everything under control, monitor him, make sure he understood what was safe and what wasn't. He was just a kid. He was my responsibility."

She frowned. "What did you do?"

"Nothing." He felt the air shrinking around him, felt it getting harder to breathe. Just like when he'd found Cal. The chill in the air around the boy's body had gotten into Sean's nose, and he'd thought he'd never be able to smell anything else ever again. He had a sharp longing for the bakery suddenly, wanting to fill his lungs with the scents of warm dough and spices. "That is, I didn't pay enough attention, and I wasn't there to keep an eye on him, and when I came to find him, he was—" He stopped, realizing his words were trailing into one another in a jumble.

"You found him?" Jess's voice was softer now.

He wanted to look at her face, but all he could see was Cal's hand, frozen in a pill-bottle shape forever. He nodded. "He overdosed. Used the paycheck I'd given him to buy a pharmacy full of stuff his new friends had recommended and tried it all at once."

"Where were you?"

Sean shook his head again, trying to come back to Jess's living room instead of that posh hotel room. "Working." He felt his lips twist into a grim line. "Once I brought him into the fold, I let him go off and have fun while I worked, worked, worked. Wanted to get that damn platinum record. He used to call me and ask if I wanted to go out."

"You said no?"

Sean nodded. "He was supposed to film a promotional spot that morning for the album. He didn't show up, so I went to find him. I was so angry. I thought … I thought he was oversleeping, hung over. I said some horrible things to him. Yelled at him. He didn't hear me."

"He was already gone?"

"He was cold, Jess. His hand—" He broke off, looking down at his own hand, which had curved into the same shape as Cal's when he'd found him. Jess's eyes followed his, and she reached out to cover his hand with her own. Her skin felt like the only warm thing in the world.

"You didn't kill him, Sean."

He barked out a bitter laugh. "That's what they keep telling me. There was an investigation and everything. They kept saying I did all I could. It's bullshit."

Jess's eyes went soft. "What happened next?"

He sighed. "I couldn't stay there. I resigned from the record company and came back home, thinking I'd work in the bakery for a few months while I decided what to do with my life."

"How long ago was that?"

"About two years," he admitted.

"What happened?"

"I had—still have, actually—these nightmares. And the only thing that made them stop…"

"Drinking?"

"Ding ding, you win." He slumped against the couch. "I pickled myself for a long time."

"Why'd you stop?"

"My friends cut me off."

She raised an eyebrow. "They were giving you the booze?"

"No, not exactly. But—Look, you met them. Between them, Max owns Frankie's, Noah owns the best vineyard in town, and Iain owns the local distillery. They called every restaurant and bar in town and blacklisted me."

"They must care for you a lot," she said quietly.

"They're good friends." If he thought about how much his friends had done for him, he might start to cry, so it was time to move on. "But I'm still the same person who was drinking, still the same person who got Cal killed. I can't ... I can't seem to get past it, Jess. And being with you is so easy. And wonderful. I feel like I don't deserve it."

She slid along the couch until her thigh bumped up against his. "You're also still the person who has dinner with his mom, and who let a complete stranger teach you to make a pie to take to your friends' house. Everyone is good *and* bad, Sean."

"The bad seems to outweigh the good," he said. He loved Jess's positive attitude, but it couldn't survive forever. Without the Jess Effect, was there any Jess? He could kill her as easily as he'd killed Cal. "I want to be with you, Jess, but I don't want to hurt you."

"I don't want you to hurt me either," she said. "But I'd rather go out trying than not have the chance."

He leaned his head on her shoulder and felt her arms come around him. "Last night I found a bottle of whiskey in my desk." Her body stiffened imperceptibly.

"What did you do?" Her voice was even, but his answer mattered. A lot. They both knew it.

"Funny thing. There was also a cookbook in the same drawer, one of my mom's old family ones. And while I was trying to ignore the whiskey staring at me, I started flipping through it. And this piece of paper fell out."

"What was on it?"

"A recipe for a whiskey glaze."

"You're kidding."

"I'm not. I'd actually been looking for a recipe for exactly that, hoping to convince my mom to change a few things at the bakery if I could prove that even our family recipes have variations. I'd given up on it before I got to this book. But there it was."

"And?"

"I took the book and the bottle both down to the bakery in the middle of the night like some sort of weirdo and left them there."

"Both of them?"

He nodded. "I'm going to talk to my mom about it, see if she'd be willing to let me try a few new things."

"So you want to stay in River Hill?" Her voice was suddenly strange, and he raised his head to look her in the eyes.

"I honestly don't know for sure, but stagnation isn't helping anybody any more than the drinking was." He'd realized last night that they were two sides of the same coin. His mother wouldn't take risks with the bakery because she didn't know what the future held; he'd gotten drunk every night because he couldn't handle his past waiting to taint his future. But neither one of them were moving forward. "I want to see what's next," he said, and let his lips meet Jess's.

A low hum rose in her throat, and he felt the Jess Effect washing over him. He smiled against her lips.

"What?" she asked, pulling back slightly.

"Nothing." Her eyes narrowed, and he laughed. "I just really like being with you. I promise that's all."

She put a hand on his chest, preventing him from kissing her again. "What about L.A.?"

"Oh!" He smacked his forehead with his hand. "That's the best part. I can't believe I didn't get to it."

"You're coming with me?"

"Actually, in a bizarre coincidence, I got an interesting email. Have you ever heard of the show 'Died Too Soon'?"

She nodded. "My sister loves it." Then her hand flew to her mouth. "Oh! Are they, um, doing an episode about Cal?"

"They're filming next Friday. And they want me to interview me for it."

Her eyebrows wrinkled together as she frowned with concern. "Are you—can you—?"

He slid an arm around Jess and pulled her up into his lap. "I think I can. I might completely fall apart on camera and start blubbering, but Cal deserves for his story to be told, and I think I can help to tell it. Especially with you around. If the offer still stands, I'd love to join you in L.A. for your audition. I'm pumped for you, and I know you're going to nail it. Getting to watch you kick ass at that audition is way more important than my freak out about going back to my old haunts. And if you're with me when I interview—" He broke off. "I need you, Jess. More than you'll ever know."

She melted against him, and he felt as though his entire body exhaled in relief. Her arms came up around his neck and her fingers tangled in his hair, and he bent his head to hers to claim her lips again.

She might be on the verge of leaving River Hill for a tremendous career opportunity, and he might be giving serious thought to staying here for the rest of his life. But he couldn't bring himself to care. A weekend in L.A. with Jess sounded like paradise. And watching her take control of her future was exactly what he needed in order to claim his own.

He couldn't think of a better place to be than by her side, for as long as she would let him.

Unless, of course, it was in her bed. Which was where they headed next.

CHAPTER 20

Suppressing a grin, Jess unclipped the wireless mic from her belt and passed the small device back to the production assistant. Jai had warned her before she'd arrived that she'd be auditioning on the actual set where the show would be filmed. Silently, she offered up a word of thanks to Sylvia Barrows for the opportunity that had led to this moment. Jess didn't want to pat herself on the back too much, but she'd nailed the audition, and she had the segments she'd done with Sylvia to thank for that. She never would have been comfortable with the director's prompts otherwise.

When she turned to exit, her eyes connected with Sean's, who was standing off to the far side waiting for her. No one outside the production team was supposed to be on the set, but when they'd pulled up to the curb earlier, Matt Combs, the head producer, had been arriving at the same time. He'd recognized Sean, and the two men had spent the next five minutes chatting about this new venture with The Beauty Network. When Sean turned to go, Matt had invited him inside. Jess could tell he'd been uncomfortable at first, but now he looked at her with so much warmth and affection that her cheeks flushed under the weight of his admiration.

"You were amazing," he mouthed from across the room.

"Thank you," she mouthed back as she made her way toward Matt and his business partner, an older gentleman who'd introduced himself as Bill Kingston. Bill would serve as executive producer, as she understood it. He made all the final decisions while Matt handled the day to day operations.

As she spoke with the two men, her eyes kept darting between Sean and the digital clock over Bill's shoulder. They were in Universal City, but Sean's interview was a few miles away in Burbank. The studios weren't that far apart, but as Jess had learned when they'd landed at LAX the day before, it could take an hour to drive even just a few miles in L.A.'s infamous traffic. Sean needed to leave soon if he was going to make it on time.

She focused her attention back on Bill, her potential boss, and he extended his hand. "Thank you again for flying down, Jess. I have a really good feeling about what we saw here today."

She smiled. "Thank you for the opportunity. I hope to hear from you soon."

"Oh, you definitely will. Now if you'll excuse me, I have a lunch date." Bill shook her hand as well, and then stalked quickly across the studio, his long, lean legs eating up the space.

Matt looked to where Sean was stationed thirty or so feet away, and his gaze turned momentarily sympathetic. "He looks good."

Jess didn't want to pry, but her curiosity about Sean's life prior to Cal's death was too hard to ignore. Matt was the only person she'd met who knew the old Sean, the one she could see now and then glimmering under the surface of this new, more somber man. "I get the impression you two were friends before …" She trailed off, unable to bring herself to say the words.

"Not friends, exactly, but we ran in the same circles. Even before the kid's death, there was talk."

A thread of unease skittered down Jess's spine. "Talk?"

Matt leaned close and dropped his voice low. "This is a work hard, play hard industry, Jess. And Sean worked hard, but he played even harder." He tapped the side of his nose twice.

A lump of unease formed in her gut. She might be naive, but she wasn't stupid. She understood exactly what he was saying. Sean had told her he hadn't used drugs, but he could have lied about that.

No, she thought vehemently. Sean had no reason to lie. He'd told her his darkest secrets and shared his harrowing pain. Cutting himself open like that only to hold something back didn't jibe with who he was. Matt was wrong about the vice, but that didn't mean he was wrong about the partying. She was about to tell him so when he took a step back and lifted his chin in greeting, his entire demeanor changing.

"Hey man. We were just talking about you."

Sean shoved his hands into his pockets and rocked back on his heels. He looked toward Jess with silent question in his deep blue gaze. He pasted a false smile on his handsome face. "Only good things, I hope."

"I was just telling Jess what a shark you were back in the day." He clapped Sean on the shoulder. "No one played the game like my man here."

Sean smiled easily at the compliment, and suddenly the lump in Jess's belly grew two sizes, pushing up against her diaphragm until she felt like she couldn't breathe. By all accounts, Sean had been happy in Los Angeles until Cal's untimely death. He'd said himself that he would never have returned home otherwise. He'd been sick to his stomach with nerves when they'd stepped off the plane yesterday, but she wondered now if running into Matt had him regretting running away and then staying away.

Was he ready to move on from his grief? Had coming here and seeing things with fresh eyes and a changed perspective altered his outlook on the situation? And if it had, was he also reconsidering her place in his life? Maybe the old Sean wouldn't want someone like her by his side. Her siblings' earlier comments came back to torment her. She wasn't like him; none of them were. They hadn't played the race card outright, but she'd understood their meaning well enough.

People like the Amorys ran River Hill, while people like her family worked for them. Her papa was the vineyard manager for Carter Bradstone. It was a prestigious position, to be sure, but he hadn't started out that way—and the people who joined in their family holiday celebrations were reflections of his humble beginnings. She'd grown up surrounded by day laborers and immigrants, some of whom she presumed were not in America legally. Even now, as an adult, she would join her grandfather at harvest time to pass out frozen treats and cold water to the men who picked the grapes that became award-winning wines that cost hundreds of dollars a bottle. Bottles they themselves could never afford, even though the Bradstones had a good reputation for how they treated their employees, thanks in no small part to Vincent Casillas' influence

Her eyes flicked back to Sean as he spoke animatedly with Matt and she chastised herself for thinking the worst. She knew this man. She knew the heart and soul of him. He cared deeply for those he let into his inner circle, and even though he'd struggled in the aftermath of Cal's death, he'd never stopped being that person. There had been moments these past couple of years where he might have lost himself a bit, but now that he was sober, he was even more committed to being a good person.

No, he wouldn't toss her aside. If she got the job and he came back to L.A. with her, they could build a life together. In fact, Jess thought it might be for the best. Her brothers weren't thrilled with the idea of her being with him, and Manny and Robert might make try to make things difficult between them. She suppressed a quick flash of rage. She didn't like Manny's new girlfriend, but she'd never once considered trying to keep them apart.

Then again, she was a woman, while her brothers considered themselves to be big, studly men. The rules that applied to her did not apply to them. Briefly, she had a faint memory of her father telling her mother that she needed to stay home and take care of their kids while he brought home the paycheck. Not that *that* had worked out all that well for them. Hmm. All this time she'd thought her brothers' attitudes stereotypical Latin machismo, but maybe it was their Irish heritage that was the problem. Or perhaps they were just men.

But manhood, and who coped with it best, was a question for another day.

She turned to Sean to remind him of the time when she caught a flash of agony spread across his face. Quickly, he suppressed it, and the conversation continued as if it had never happened. But Jess knew she hadn't imagined the ticking of his jaw or the panicked way his eyes had darted toward the door. She focused back in on their conversation to hear Matt recounting all the plans they'd had for Cal Grissom and excitedly explaining how they didn't have to go to waste. There was another young kid he thought could slot right in—if he had the right producer. Again, Matt's meaning was more than clear: Sean could groom the kid's look and sound, while he would give him a global stage via carefully selected television spots.

With one more look at Sean, she pushed all her daydreams for them aside. He'd never teach her to surf out at Huntington Beach. They'd never visit his favorite out-of-the-way Mexican restaurant (which he'd told her in confidence served even better tacos than Frankie's). And they'd certainly never hop in the car and drive up to Vegas for a weekend of naked debauchery.

He couldn't be here. Not if it meant his demons pushing in on him from every angle. No, he was better off in River Hill, where he had his friends and his family's bakery … and most important of all, his sobriety.

So where did that leave them?

Counting chickens, Jess.

She pasted on a smile she didn't feel and turned to him, laying a hand on his arm. "We should get going if you're going to make your appointment."

He nodded once and then shook Matt's hand. "It was good seeing you."

"You too. Let's get drinks the next time you're in town."

If Matt noticed that Sean let the invite hang between them without a response, he didn't comment on it.

"You ready to head back to the hotel?" His voice was flat, and all the warmth she'd seen as he'd whispered at her from across the room had disappeared.

Jess flicked uncertain eyes between his. "Will you have time to come up, or …" She felt the need to be close to him. They'd had sex that morning in their room's oversized walk-in shower, but she wanted a bed and a few moments of quiet intimacy to connect. She'd ended her audition feeling like everything was finally going her way, but that had all changed in twenty minutes. If she got the job and moved down to L.A., there was a genuine possibility that she'd lose

Sean. She couldn't ask him to come back to this place. Not after seeing how it affected him.

He set his hand to the small of her back and guided her toward the exit. "Nah. I'll drop you off, and then head straight over to the studio for the interview."

"Oh, okay." She tried not to let her disappointment show as he opened her car door and she slid inside.

When he climbed into the driver's seat, he gripped the steering wheel tight. After a few quiet moments in which Jess watched him physically pull himself together, his vice-like grip eased, and he turned his face toward hers. "Be careful with him."

"Who, Matt?"

He nodded once, his lips flattening into a tight line. "He can be unpredictable."

Unpredictable was not a word you wanted to describe the man who you were about to work for. Assuming, of course, he hired her. Both Matt and Bill had been pleased by her audition, and Matt had indicated Jai would be hearing from him soon. But if Sean didn't think he could be trusted, was he just blowing smoke up her ass to keep her on the hook while they decided if something better might come along?

Suddenly, she missed Marisol. Her sister might be the most difficult woman in all of Christendom, but Jess knew deep down Marisol had her back and would give it to her straight. Maybe her family had been right, and she did actually need one of them by her side. Not as a chaperone, but rather, as a cheering squad.

Sean flipped on the blinker and pulled out of the parking lot into mid-day traffic. He flicked his eyes toward hers as he navigated into the far-left lane. "He knows the business inside and out, but his top priority is making sure the people he works with are seen by all the people that matter, when and where it matters."

That was just good business, Jess thought. No matter what industry you were in, you needed to make a name for yourself. In Hollywood, that meant knowing the right people. With Jai in her corner, she was already off to a good start. She didn't love Matt as a person, but she'd done her research. Everything he touched turned to gold. Working for him would be a good thing. Wouldn't it?

"Can I ask you something?" She shifted in her seat to better read his facial expressions while they spoke. Not that he was giving her much beyond a deep scowl.

"Of course."

"What aren't you telling me?"

He pulled into the hotel's parking lot and instead of navigating to the front where he could drop Jess off and make a quick getaway, he pulled into a vacant spot and killed the engine. "What do you mean?" he asked, turning to face her, his back pressed against the door.

"I thought the audition went really well, and it seemed like you were happy for me. What's changed?" She hadn't imagined the look on his face when he'd told her how amazing she'd been. There'd been genuine pride there.

"You were fantastic. Don't ever doubt that. But Matt ..." His eyes darted away, and he fidgeted in his seat.

"But Matt what?"

His gaze found hers again, and the expression on his face nearly stole her breath. Something about the other man caused Sean legitimate pain. She leaned forward and palmed both his knees. "Please, tell me."

"You remember he used to work for The Music Channel?" She nodded, and he continued. "I don't know if you picked up on it, but Matt was one of the execs we'd tapped to help with Cal's debut. I don't have any proof, but I do know for a fact that Matt has hooked other stars up with drugs. He was a huge coke fiend himself when I knew him."

Jess's blood ran cold as Sean gripped her hands in his. "That's … that's terrible. How could he do something like that?" Jess wasn't as naive as her siblings liked to claim—she knew there was a seedy underbelly of Hollywood—she just hadn't wanted to think that she'd potentially be working with someone who was in the thick of it.

He rubbed his thumb over her knuckles. "Like I said, I don't have any proof, I just … I really don't like being around people who were part of that scene. I never thought I'd say this, but I can't wait to get home. Back to River Hill." He let loose a huff that was part laugh, part dismay, and shook his head.

Jess's heart broke for him. While she'd loved spending the past day and a half with him away from the stress and pressure of their everyday lives—and had definitely appreciated the support he'd shown her today—it wasn't healthy for him to be here. As soon as his interview with 'Died Too Soon' wrapped, she was going to suggest they fly home tonight instead of on Sunday as planned. And all those long, lazy weekends exploring Southern California together she'd been envisioning? Yeah, those were off the table too. Suddenly, her dream job in L.A. didn't seem so dream-like.

She twined their fingers together and raised one of his hands to her lips. "Do you want me to come with you to the taping?"

"I'm … it's—" his eyes flicked between hers, and he blew out a long breath "—are you sure you want to see that? It's probably going to get ugly."

"I want whatever you want. Just tell me what you need."

"I need you, Jess. Just you."

She nodded once, acknowledging what those words really meant. The world could be an ugly, lonely place, but she was his safe haven. The problem was, that was a lot of pressure to place on one person and a new relationship. She was falling in love with Sean, but she didn't know if she was strong enough for him. She also didn't know if he was strong enough for *her*. She'd done a lot of growing since they'd met, and she'd finally started to come into her own. Not to mention her new career prospects.

Suddenly, Jess had a lot to think about.

CHAPTER 21

Sean eased himself onto the wooden stool and took a moment to let the reality of where he was and what he was about to do wash over him. Thank goodness this studio was calmer than the one Jess had auditioned at; he wasn't sure he could have handled being assaulted by all that energy. He was enjoying the faint air of academia that seemed to permeate the 'Died Too Soon' set. When he arrived, he'd been greeted by somebody who'd called himself a 'staff researcher.' The man had *literally* been wearing a tweed jacket.

Now, as he looked around and saw busy people doing their jobs, he felt himself relaxing. He'd been greeted warmly by several of the other interviewees, old friends and colleagues he'd left behind in his rush to escape L.A. Not one of them had asked him to have a drink with them afterward. Although he had been asked out for a coffee and another had asked him for a recipe for scones. It was as though they knew about his problem and were being sensitive to it. Not what he'd expected from his old crowd. It made him wonder if he'd jumped ship too fast. Maybe he should have stayed, gotten help, moved on.

His eyes strayed to the back of the room, where Jess stood chatting with one of the sound techs. Her beauty shone in the bustling room, easy to find in the crowd of headset-wearing film people.

"Are you ready?" The PA was a curvaceous woman who wore horn-rimmed glasses under a messy bun of rich honey-brown hair. Her name was Margo, he thought. Possibly Margaret. Mildred? She was pleasant enough, but efficiency was her middle name. He suspected that she was what made this entire operation run as smoothly as it did.

"I think so," he said.

"Okay. Just to double check, you understand what's going to happen?"

He nodded. "That person over there's going to clip a mic on me, and that lady right there's going to film me while that guy prompts me with the questions that your research team put together."

She nodded. "And you had a chance to go over the questions before you got here, right?"

"Yeah, somebody emailed them to me. Thanks for that, by the way."

She grinned, lighting her face up in an unexpected way. "You're welcome. We're not practicing 'gotcha journalism' over here. We don't want to surprise you with anything. It's a collaborative effort. We want you to be able to speak effectively, preferably at length, so we have a lot of material to pull from for the final cut. Can't do that if you're blinking at the camera like a surprised fish after getting blindsided by something you weren't expecting."

"That makes a lot of sense." After he'd sent the email agreeing to be interviewed on the show, everything had happened very quickly. But every touchpoint between him and the show's staff had been handled with both thoroughness and sensitivity. No wonder people had been so complimentary online.

A tall man who looked as though he would be right at home wearing the staff researcher's tweed jacket approached them. "Hi, Sean, I'm Graham Parvis. Executive producer."

"Nice to meet you."

"You too, man." Graham stuck his hand out, and Sean shook it. "I just thought I'd come over and say thank you for coming."

"You greet everyone personally?" Sean asked, letting a smirk cross his lips.

Graham chuckled. "Just the ones who seem a little gun-shy. We specialize in getting people who wouldn't otherwise speak out to come on our show. Sometimes it seems like it helps them a little bit." He grinned. "Not nearly as much as it helps us, of course."

"Ah, a gentle mercenary," Sean laughed. "You must be quite an attraction at parties." He suspected that Graham Parvis didn't generally fit into the Hollywood scene.

The other man smiled. "You've got me. I'm not great at the social part of this job. That's why I was so glad this show got greenlit. I got to build a whole staff of people just like me." He waved an arm to encompass the entire studio.

Sean leaned forward, the words coming out impulsively. "You know, if you ever have time, you should come to River Hill. I think you'd like it." Now that he'd been away for a couple of years, he could recognize a fellow Hollywood outcast. And for the first time in his life, he was proud to tell people about River Hill, proud to hail from the tiny Northern California town where good food, great whiskey, and fantastic wine came from. Standing here now, he felt downright appreciative to have called it home.

Graham regarded him solemnly. "Thanks, man. Maybe I

will."

The sound guy moved in, and the producer moved away as Sean got mic'd and sound tested. And then it began.

The first few questions were simple. He told them his name, and what his job had been. He described his duties as a producer and recounted the moment he'd first seen Cal's videos online. The joy that the kid had managed to imbue in his music had been infectious, and Sean had known he needed to get on a plane to meet him as soon as he could.

Things became a little harder to discuss when he had to start talking about how he'd recruited Cal. He acknowledged that it was standard procedure to overwhelm potential clients with the possibilities of L.A., all tailored to their age and interests. And nineteen-year-old boys had pretty standard interests. Cal hadn't been an exception.

After signing on the dotted line, he'd moved to L.A. and Sean had helped him get an apartment. They'd begun laying down tracks around the same time as Cal had started to explore his new home and the benefits tied to his new paycheck.

"Did you try to steer him away from the parties?" The interviewer asked quietly. His tone was even, no judgment. But Sean didn't need external judgment. He knew what he'd done.

He could feel himself start to sweat. "Not enough," he said. His voice was shaking, so he cleared his throat and said it again. "Not enough. I went back to work. I didn't pay enough attention to what he was doing, who he was with. I just focused on the album. It was a mistake. The worst I've ever made."

The interviewer nodded blandly. "What happened?"

He'd told the story to Jess once. The sky hadn't fallen. He looked up. Sought her out in the crowd of silent listeners. Nobody's face wore anything but gentle support, but hers blazed with pride, sympathy, and determination. He watched her mouth *you can do this.*

He *could* do this. He took a deep breath and told his story. "I felt responsible for a long time. I still do, honestly. They did an investigation, which revealed I hadn't done anything wrong, but in my heart, I know I failed Cal. He was a talented kid, and he was my friend, and I didn't do enough to help him. I've had to live with that every day, and I haven't handled it well." He let out a dry chuckle. "That's the understatement of the year. I drank. Nearly drank myself to death. I don't know how everyone else on the team handled Cal's death, because I ran away. I'm from a small town a few hours away, and my family runs a bakery. I went home, and I worked in the bakery, and I drank until I couldn't see straight anymore, and I still saw him every time I closed my eyes." If you were going to confess your sins, you might as well do it in front of cameras for national audience viewing, right?

"I didn't come up for air until some good friends forced me to, and I've started to learn the lesson that Cal's life should have taught me all along. Seize the joy and stay with the people you love. Don't run from your past; it'll only haunt your future."

"And now?" The interviewer's voice broke the silence in the room.

"Now, I'm ready to have a future again. I'll think about Cal a lot, still, I know. But I'm going to try to remember him as he was in life, and I'll mourn the loss of what we could have seen from him, while still appreciating the time we had."

"Will you be coming back to the recording industry?"

Sean shook his head. "This has been a great trip in a lot of ways, and I have to thank you folks for bringing me back to L.A. I was terrified, thinking that I'd immediately do something wrong, and fail myself or somebody else. But I'm remembering that I have some good friends here, too, which is great. I think I'll be visiting occasionally, but my home now is River Hill." He let his grin grow. "You might have heard of it recently. It's a great town. I can recommend the bakery."

Chuckles from the staff members serving as the studio audience followed that, and he hoped they kept it in the final cut. "I'm ready for what's next," he said firmly and raised his eyes to find Jess, to show her that he meant what he'd said.

She was gone.

He let the sound tech unclip him, shook hands with the crew and his old friends, made promises to keep in touch, all while looking around the studio. She really wasn't here. She'd left him.

He made his way back to their hotel, anxiety growing in the pit of his stomach while he tried to ignore it. Maybe she'd left early to come back here to take a nap. Or maybe she was hungry, had stepped out for lunch.

He slipped his keycard into the lock, and as the faint click of the door sounded, his phone buzzed.

Jess: I took an earlier flight. Have a lot to do. Sorry.

The door clicked again, indicating it had re-locked itself because he'd taken too long to turn the handle. He barely heard it.

She'd just … left?

Not just the studio, not just the building. Not for lunch, or a nap. She'd left him here in L.A., alone. And flown back to River Hill without him.

He finally managed to get the door open with shaking hands. He made his way inside and sat down on the bed with a thump. They hadn't even managed to have sex in it; steamy shower sex, sure, but he'd been looking forward to laying her down and spending tonight savoring her body. Apparently, she hadn't felt the same.

Hearing him talk about what he'd done and how he'd failed Cal again must have made her realize that he was too much to handle. He put his head in his hands. He was trying so hard to turn himself into a better man. Not just for himself, but for her. She deserved somebody who could support her unequivocally, without turning into a nervous wreck the second anyone innocently offered him a glass of wine. She'd fucking nailed that audition. If they didn't give her the hosting gig, he'd be shocked. Maybe she'd realized that her new career opportunity wasn't a good fit for her small-town boyfriend.

She'd been surprised by his revelation about Matt's history, but even he knew that it wasn't enough to keep her from taking the job. And if he were honest with himself, he suspected that Matt had been far more on the straight and narrow since Cal's death. They'd all been impacted in different ways. Matt was still a wheeler and dealer in the business sense of the words, but the brief rumors Sean had heard all indicated that the partying had been toned way down. He still didn't have to like the guy, though.

How could he expect Jess to tether herself to somebody who could barely stand to be in L.A. for more than a day when she probably expected to move here? *Oh, God.* That was it. That was why she'd left. She was a lot faster on the uptake than he was. She was moving to L.A. He'd just publicly committed to staying in River Hill.

How could they possibly make this work?

He'd tried so hard to make himself a better man lately, but she needed more from him. He needed more from himself. But he wasn't sure he had it in him. He rubbed his hands over his face, then froze as realization hit him. He was thinking of solutions, of ways he could work on himself and his relationships. He wasn't thinking about alcohol at *all*.

Sean stood and began throwing his things back into his weekender bag. He'd be damned if he wasn't going to try. He might be broken, but he loved her. There had to be a way.

CHAPTER 22

Swish, thump, swish, thump. Jess's footfalls echoed in her head as her feet met asphalt. *Swish, thump, coward. Swish thump, coward.*

She'd left him. She'd gotten up out of her seat and walked straight out of the studio, back to the hotel where she'd haphazardly thrown her belongings into her carry-on bag, and then to the airport. Like a coward.

At the time, it had seemed the wisest course of action was to give herself some space to think without the weight of her feelings for Sean coloring her perspective. And for a minute or two, it had worked. But then she'd gotten a call from Jai as her plane had touched down in Oakland offering her the job, and she'd begun spiraling all over again.

And now that she was back in River Hill, all she felt was guilt. Guilt for being unsupportive when Sean had been the exact opposite. Guilt for leaving him in his moment of need. And guilt for wanting two things that seemed diametrically opposed to one another. No doubt, she was falling in love with him, but she was also in love with the idea of launching a career her family couldn't mock. Beauty-queen-turned-

175

beauty-blogger had a limited shelf life, and Jess didn't know what she would do once its expiration date came due. But beauty-queen-turned-TV-host opened up a whole host of opportunities she'd never considered.

Just look at Tyra Banks and Heidi Klum. Not that Jess considered herself on the famous supermodels' level by any stretch of the imagination. Or rather, Marisol wouldn't let her consider it. When she'd spoken with her sister this morning, Jess had floated the idea that she could parlay her minor fame into a strong, steady career on award-winning shows like theirs. It was at that point her sister had given her the patented Marisol "are you fucking with me?" glare and thrown out another name: Kate Plimpton, a fellow former Miss Teen USA contestant who'd botched an answer about U.S. geography so badly that she'd achieved instant notoriety. Two years later, she'd ended up as a contestant on World Traveler Challenge, but no one had heard from her since. They'd looked her up online to find that she was now selling real estate a couple of miles away from where Jess had auditioned.

All in all, not a bad life, but not the one Jess imagined for herself, either. Marisol, however, thought Jess going into real estate was the perfect solution to her career crisis. To hear Marisol tell it, all of Jess's years as a pageant queen—smiling and nodding at people she'd rather yell at—was excellent preparation for dealing with clients. Her sister had even offered to set Jess up with a friend who sold houses in the next county over. She'd politely declined.

And after *that* conversation, Jess had gone running. She'd needed to. If she didn't work off some of her excess nerves and frustration, she was liable to head straight to the closest restaurant and order every dessert on their menu. Since she was trying *not* to vomit, that seemed like a terrible idea.

As she came around a bend in the road, the valley

opened up in front of her, and her stride faltered. When she'd left her house an hour ago, she hadn't had a set route, but she'd never intended to run this far. Jess slowed her pace and tapped the screen on her watch. Twelve-point-five miles. *Holy cow!* She'd once run a half marathon for charity, and when she'd crossed the finish line, she'd wanted to fall down and never get up again. Another half a mile and she'd match that distance. Unfortunately, that meant by the time she ran home, she'd have run a *full* marathon—and that wasn't something she was ready for. No matter how many nerves she had propelling her forward.

Jess dropped forward at the waist and slapped her palms to her thighs. Pulling a deep breath into her lungs, she looked around at her surroundings. She'd never run this way before, but if she wasn't mistaken, this was the same road Sean had taken the night he'd pulled his truck off the road and into a stretch of vines. Jess stood and shielded her eyes. Spinning around in a circle, she got her bearings. Yeah, this was the place. No wonder he hadn't been worried about someone calling the cops on them for trespassing. This was Noah Bradstone's land, and just up ahead, half a mile beyond was Angelica Travis's bed and breakfast, where Jess had first met Jai.

Jess hated to drop in unannounced, especially looking sweaty and disheveled, but she hadn't been prepared to run quite so far. Putting one foot in front of the other, she jogged the rest of the way to The Oakwell Inn, hitting the driveway just as a car was pulling in. Jess stopped to let the guest pull in ahead of her when the driver stopped the vehicle and rolled down the window.

"Jess?"

"Yes?" She shielded her eyes again. "Oh, hey."

Naomi Klein lifted her sunglasses. "Are you okay?"

"Yes, why?" Her question came out as a high-pitched squeak. "I'm fine."

"Are you sure? Because you look like you're about to die of heat stroke. And you're covered in road dust."

Jess glanced down to see that her ankles were three shades darker than her normal skin tone. Sweat dripped down her temple, and she wiped her brow with her forearm—which came away streaked with dirt and grime. "Shit."

An awkward silence hung between them for a few beats, and then Naomi said, "I'm heading up to the inn for book club. Do you want to rinse off there and join us?"

Caught off guard at the other woman's invitation, Jess's response came out a flustered jumble of platitudes. "Oh, no. I couldn't. I mean, thank you. That's very nice. I mean, it's not nice. It's—" She blew out a breath and shook her head. Putting on her best smile, she said, "Sorry. Thank you for the invitation, but I couldn't."

"Sure, you could."

"I don't even know what book you're covering."

Naomi chuckled. "If it makes you feel any better, we spend about ten minutes discussing the book, and the next two hours gossiping and drinking Noah's wine."

Jess chewed her lip. She could use a drink of water—and a toilet, if she were honest—but she didn't want to intrude so far as to beg the use of a shower. Especially not with the way she looked. She didn't know what kind of furniture The Oakwell Inn had, but she pictured it all white and shabby chic and she was a mess. Definitely a bad combination.

As if sensing her hesitancy, Naomi upped the ante. "I've got a spare outfit in the trunk you can borrow. And if you come in, we'll tell you everything you want to know about Sean."

Jess sucked in a breath. She'd hoped her run would banish thoughts of him, but it hadn't worked. And now, hearing his name spoken aloud was a painful reminder of how she'd failed him. She needed to apologize, but not just *any* apology. It had to be a get-down-on-your-knees-and-grovel sort of apology. The type of "please forgive me for how stupid I've been" that he wouldn't be able to ignore. Maybe his friends could help her figure out how to do that. Because she didn't have the first clue where to start.

"I see you waffling. You know you want to." Naomi laughed, and Jess grinned despite herself.

"Yeah, okay."

"Climb in, and we'll drive the rest of the way. You look like you're about to fall over."

* * *

FORTY MINUTES LATER, Jess emerged from a steamy bathroom wrapped in one of the inn's plush white robes with a towel on her head. Angelica had taken one look at Jess and pushed her into a white marble room with orders not to come out until she felt better. At first, Jess had been offended, but then Maeve Brennan—Naomi's boyfriend's little sister and part-owner of the town's famous distillery—had sauntered past and informed Jess that this was Angelica's *thing*. Apparently, the gorgeous blonde Amazon thought a hot bubble bath was the best cure for whatever ails you. Both Maeve and Naomi had been shoved in there a time or two.

As it turned out, Angelica was right. Jess felt infinitely better than when she'd walked in. She changed into the clothes Naomi had left for her and joined the other women in a sunlit room decorated in shades of white, sage green, and white-washed wood. She curled up on a sofa—white linen, just as she'd imagined—while the others passed a bottle of red wine between them.

Angelica held it aloft, and Jess shook her head. She wasn't

a big drinker to begin with, but since finding out about Sean's struggle with sobriety, she hadn't had a single drop of alcohol. It hadn't been a conscious decision; just something that had happened naturally.

"Sparkling water instead?"

"Yes, please."

Angelica leaned forward, picked up a pitcher from the coffee table, and poured Jess a glass, topping it with a thin slice of lime. Passing it to Maeve, who in turn passed it to Jess, she said, "This week's book is about a young woman who falls for an older, sexy man who has a dark past. He's difficult and surly, but her love saves him. Do you have any thoughts on that, Jess?"

Jess nearly spit out her water. "Um …"

"A *very* fascinating story," Naomi interjected with a knowing smile. "Don't you think?"

Jess's head swiveled to Maeve, who was holding her hands up in a sign of surrender. "Don't look at me. I'm just here for the wine and the man candy."

"Speaking of man candy," Angelica continued breezily, "how are things going with Sean?"

Jess's eyes darted to Naomi. "You!" She pointed at the tall brunette. "You lured me here under false pretenses." She didn't know whether to laugh or cry. This sneak attack would be hilarious if it were happening to someone else.

Naomi chuckled. "I did no such thing. Wine—" she lifted her glass to her lips and took a drink. "And gossip." She gestured at Jess as if to say, 'get on with it.'

"You said you'd tell me everything I wanted to know about Sean."

Angelica settled back in her deep, overstuffed chair. "And we will. Just as soon as you tell us how things are going." The other woman stared at her intently, and Jess got the impression there was more to her question than she was letting on.

She looked between Angelica, Naomi, and Maeve, and she *knew* there was. "You know what happened."

Naomi and Angelica both nodded while Maeve shook her head. "Not me, but now I want to." Her eyes sparkled with interest.

Jess didn't know these women. Heck, it was the first time she'd ever met Maeve, but she'd felt drawn to the small redhead almost instantly. Jess and Maeve were closer in age than she was with Naomi and Angelica, which might have had something to do with it. That, and Maeve's infectious grin and happy, sing-songy lilt. She couldn't say why, but she just knew the Irish girl would be a good friend to have.

Something she was in short supply of.

Jess had hundreds of *acquaintances*, but no one—save Marisol—who she could call for advice or a nice long chat. And given how recent conversations with her sister had gone, she wasn't sure that was such a good thing. There'd been a few times she'd wondered if being an orphan might have been simpler.

But *these* women were lovely. Nosy, but lovely. Immediately, they'd welcomed her into their fold and made her feel accepted. And goodness, how she longed to be accepted. All she had to do in return was confess her sins— something she did one Sunday a month anyhow.

She looked at Maeve and winced as she confessed. "I abandoned him in L.A."

Maeve, in turn, looked to Angelica and Naomi.

"One of his proteges died on his watch, and he fled for home a couple of years ago," Naomi explained. "He hadn't been back until this past weekend."

"Oh."

"Yeah, oh." Jess felt her face growing hot as she continued. "I don't know what happened. All I can say in my defense is that I panicked. I'd just come from an audition for an amazing new job, and I had all these conflicting thoughts swirling around in my head. At first, I'd hoped he might be able to move down to L.A. with me, but then I saw how hard it was for him to be there, and I knew that was asking too much." She pulled in a deep breath, and then let it out slowly as she tried to get a grip on her emotions. "Then, at the taping of the show he was doing about Cal's death, I realized that he belonged in River Hill. He's happy here. And that's when I panicked."

Angelica nodded sagely. "That's what he said happened."

Jess's head shot up. "He did?"

Angelica's lips flattened into a thoughtful line. "He thought you were panicking about *him*."

Jess's head whipped from side to side in denial. "No, never about him. I love him." She stopped short, her eyes going wide. "I love him," she whispered with wonder. The declaration was startling, but not untrue. She couldn't say when she'd crossed over the imaginary line from falling into fallen, but it had definitely happened. "I love him, and I abandoned him."

Naomi took a sip of wine, seemingly undaunted. "A page out of my playbook, then."

Maeve laughed and shook her head. "You didn't abandon my brother so much as run away screaming."

Naomi winced. "In my defense, the idea of falling in love with a man who lived in another country was terrifying."

Maeve wagged her finger at her brother's girlfriend. "Oh no, you don't. You ran even *after* you found out he was sticking around."

Naomi's cheeks turned red, and she sighed. "Yeah, I did. Thank goodness your brother doesn't put up with my bullshit."

"Your bullshit?" Jess asked, curious to find out how Naomi had managed to make things right with the Irishman.

"I'm a notorious commitment-phobe. Iain's the only man I've ever been in a relationship with. We've been together for a year—"

"Longer if you count all those months you were just having fun," Maeve interjected, using her fingers to make air quotes around that last part.

Naomi chuckled. "Okay, fine. A year and a half."

"And she still freaks out from time to time," Angelica added. "She's taken at least six baths in that room." She pointed to the large bathroom Jess had occupied herself less than half an hour ago.

Jess felt her anxiety begin to melt away. Not that she felt any less guilty about what she'd done to Sean, but at least now she had hope they might be able to see their way past it. "How did you get Iain to forgive you?"

Naomi tossed her a sly look. "First, I asked him to move in with me, and then I fucked his brains out."

Maeve set her glass down and slapped her palms over her ears. "Ew, I don't need to know what you and my brother do in the privacy of your own home."

Naomi looked toward Angelica, and the two women smirked.

"And all around town, too," Angelica said, a dreamy look coming over her face.

Jess's cheeks heated at the open and honest way they were discussing their sex lives. She'd never had that. Aside from Marisol telling her she either needed to pull the stick out of her ass or get fucked, this sort of banter had been absent from her life. Beauty queens were supposed to be sweet, prim, and proper role models. You simply did not hint to *anyone* that the man you were in love with had made you come in the front seat of his truck while parked on the side of the road.

No, not on the side of the road.

With a shy laugh, she turned to Angelica. "In your fiancé's vineyard."

Angelica barked out a laugh. "I knew it! I told Noah I saw Bessie Blue slinking down the rear drive."

Jess covered her face with her hands. "Oh, my god."

Maeve patted her knee. "Don't be ashamed. At least you're getting some. I've got tumbleweeds in my pants. If the right guy walked into this room right now and propositioned me, I'd climb up on that table and tell him to have his dirty way with me."

Jess pulled her hands away from her face and looked at Maeve with shock. Talking about your sex life was one thing; actually having sex in front of people you knew was an entirely other thing.

The Irish pixie chuckled and held up her e-reader. "Chapter ten of this week's book."

At which point they all dissolved into laughter.

By the time Iain and Noah walked in an hour later, Jess felt better than she had in days. She couldn't say how, but deep in her bones, she knew everything would be all right.

It had to be. Jess had finally found her place in the world. Sean—and by extension, these women—were smack-dab in the center of it.

CHAPTER 23

There were only so many smug text messages from Angelica that Sean could bring himself to read before he snapped and headed for The Oakwell Inn. But he had one stop to make along the way, and it didn't even involve any driving.

"You got a minute?" He poked his head into his mother's office, listening to the hum of her scanner as it finished a page.

"Sure." She put the book she was scanning aside, carefully smoothing a hand over the pages to keep it open and the pages flat. "What's up?"

"I want to take you up on those cooking lessons." He took a deep breath. "And the rest of it, too."

She was silent for a moment, observing him carefully. "You've decided to stay?"

"Long-term," he confirmed. "I want to keep baking, stay here in River Hill. Maybe work with some people I know to make a few changes, both at the bakery and in town."

"Changes, huh?"

"You know Iain Brennan? I was thinking we could use his

whiskey in the glaze for the fritters. I even found an Amory recipe for it."

"I tried one of your Mexican wedding cookies," his mother said. "There were a few left over."

"And?"

She smiled. "They're delicious. I think we should start selling them. And if you have more ideas in that vein, I'd love to hear those too."

"I'm hoping I can recapture my source of inspiration," he said, his mind roving ahead to the inn where Angelica had texted him that she, Naomi, and Maeve had captured Jess and intended to hold her for dinner. What he did with the information, she'd said, was up to him. But there was extra food.

He hadn't regretted calling Noah and blurting out his sins on speakerphone last night for a single second.

"I'd like to meet your muse," his mother said.

He grinned. "You'll like her."

"So, not a tapeworm after all, huh?"

"Not a tapeworm."

* * *

HE PARKED Bessie Blue in The Oakwell Inn's graveled parking lot alongside Naomi's car. He'd swung into the bakery to pick up some pastries for the crowd, and then he'd stopped at the farm stand nearby to pick up some fruit for Jess's dessert. The perfectly ripe pineapple smelled as sweet as the frangipane tarts. He patted his stomach, where once upon a time a defined six pack had lived. These days, he was a little less cut than he used to be. It might be good to join Jess on her side of the carb-free fence for a while.

He heard laughter coming from the kitchen when he pushed the door open. He smiled, realizing that his friends had the same effect on him that Jess did. He just hadn't let them in until now. Maybe he should re-dub it the Friend Effect and save the Jess Effect for naked time. As long as she would let him, anyway.

He pushed past the nerves bubbling in his gut. When Angelica had texted him, she'd told him he had a shot. More than a shot. Jess was here, and she wanted to see him. He wanted desperately to see her, too.

"I brought dessert," he said as he entered the kitchen.

A chorus of 'oooohs' greeted him, but he was only interested in one voice.

"Hi," she said.

"Hi."

Angelica nudged Noah. "Let's go set the table."

"We'll help you carry, uh, the forks," Iain said. He handed Naomi a single fork, and she smothered laughter as she rose and carried it ostentatiously out of the room. Maeve rolled her eyes at Jess and Sean before following the others.

"I'm sorry," he blurted once they were alone, realizing that she'd said the same thing at the same time.

"I didn't mean to scare you off." He took her hand.

"I shouldn't have run," she replied. "I panicked, to be honest."

"About me?"

"No! God, no, Sean." She brought her other hand up to encase his in both of hers. "Never. I know you."

"But—"

"I freaked out because I couldn't imagine hurting you by bringing you to L.A., and I don't want to give you up," she said frankly. "It might be selfish, but it's true."

"I don't want to give you up either," he said. "But the job—"

"I got it."

He pumped his free hand in the air. "Hell yeah, you did. I knew you would." He grinned at her, then sobered. "But—"

She slid her hands from his, squeezing it just before they came apart. "I'm not going to sacrifice my career for you, Sean."

"You shouldn't," he said as his stomach sank.

But she was continuing. "I'm not going to sacrifice you, either. Or my family. Honestly, I'm not sure I'm the sort of person who could live in L.A. full time, career or no career. I want to push forward, but I want to do it on my terms."

He raised his eyebrows, impressed. "You sound like you have a plan."

She grinned. "Actually, it's Naomi's fault. Or maybe Angelica's." She paused, thoughtfully. "Probably both. Maeve might be involved, too. You could even blame my sister if you wanted to create a sort of anti-hero for the story."

"You joined their book club, didn't you?"

She laughed. "It's a damned good book club."

"So what do you want to do? I—I love you, Jess. But I'm all in on River Hill, now." He quirked his lips into a smile. "I just announced it on TV, so it must be true."

She grinned. "Noah told me." She sobered. "You love me?"

"I love you." He didn't falter this time, so he repeated it for good measure. "I love you, Jess."

Her smile was brighter than the sunrise he saw every day during his shift at the bakery. "I love you, too."

"Can we make this work?" He shifted their bodies to fit his arms around her waist, resting his forehead against hers and feeling her warm breath on his chin.

"We can do anything we want," she whispered.

"Are you clothed?" Angelica's voice rang out, but she didn't wait for them to answer before she sailed back into the kitchen.

"If we weren't, what would you have done?" Sean asked.

"Had a pleasant surprise," she answered saucily. "Scootch; I need to take the chickens out of the oven."

He took Jess's hand, and they escaped to the dining room, where the others were waiting.

"Did you tell him about the plan?" Maeve asked, practically bouncing in her chair.

"Not completely," Jess said. "We had a few other things to cover."

"Ooey-gooey lovey-dovey stuff," Naomi said. "Yuck."

"What are you, twelve?" Iain asked. "You say that 'lovey-dovey' stuff all the time."

"Sure, but I don't tell anybody about it," she said. "I've got a reputation to uphold, here."

Sean snorted. "Pretty sure that ship sailed once Iain moved into Fortress Klein." Naomi had famously not allowed most people into her home, where she also had a studio.

"We're talking about you, not me," Naomi said primly. "And Jess, who is on the way to being the next Big Face Of TV." She made jazz hands around her face.

Sean felt the pinch of anxiety again. But Jess said she had a plan. Noah and Angelica made their thing work, but Sean didn't relish the idea of months without Jess while she was off filming like Angelica did. He'd do it if that's what she wanted. He'd do anything she wanted. Maybe he could visit. Visiting L.A. was a far cry from living there, and he'd meant what he'd said during his interview— he'd like to get back in touch with some of his old friends.

Jess held up a hand. "Can we not get ahead of ourselves?"

Angelica shook her head. "We're not getting ahead. We talked about this, Jess. You have all the leverage, here."

Jess turned to Sean. "Naomi reminded me the same thing that Jai told me a few days ago. I'm not just the girl who auditioned who was the best fit. I'm a recognizable brand."

"With millions of followers online," Naomi added. "Your

blog is amazing. Changed my approach to eyebrows completely."

"Angelica pointed out that I have a lot of leverage to negotiate how the show is filmed."

Sean nodded. "You could do what she does."

Jess shook her head. "Not quite what she does."

Angelica sniffed. "Works for me."

Jess grinned. "You're a role model, but we're not supposed to blindly follow people, right? I think my sixth-grade teacher told me that."

Angelica waved her hands. "Whatever."

Jess turned back to Sean as Noah started carving the roast chickens. "I'm going to talk to them about a couple of options. There's plenty of studio space here that they could rent—it's a new show, and a new network, so it's not like they have a lot of campus space they're trying to use up. Sylvia Barrows from the morning show has a lot of leverage with her station, and she likes me. I could probably hook them up. And if that doesn't work, we'll shoot in short bursts. I'll be gone for a day or two here and there. But the bulk of my work will be done here, researching, prepping, and exploring additional opportunities to grow the scope of the show."

Sean stared at her. "You came up with all of that in two hours of book club?"

"We also discussed some very important romance novel scenes," Maeve said.

He shook his head. "River Hill is a strange place."

"It's home," Jess said simply. Her hand curved into his again. "I might grow, and change, but I don't want to leave."

"Neither do I."

As they ate and chatted, Sean found himself slotted into a dynamic that was at once familiar and unfamiliar. These were his friends, the people he'd chosen to spend time with for years. But somehow, it was different. Sean-and-Jess was a different part of the group than Just-Sean. He stole a glance at Maeve, the only single member of their dinner party now, and wondered if it ever bothered her. If it did, he suspected she wouldn't turn to drinking like he had.

He noticed that Jess didn't have a glass of wine, though the others all had one. Nobody had offered him any, but they weren't trying to be secretive about their drinks either. He appreciated their silence on the matter, but he loved Jess. And she loved him. He was still marveling about that little fact when dessert was set on the table. Somebody had sliced up the fruit, and he handed it to Jess before taking a few pieces from the platter for himself. She shot him an appreciative glance, and his gaze fell to her water glass. A grin crossed his lips, and she smiled back, a small, secret lifting of her lips. She squeezed his hand knowingly. They were a team.

He drove her home later, after hearing about the running snafu that had brought her to Angelica's in the first place. In borrowed clothes, she'd seemed a little embarrassed about the situation, but he could only be glad of the excuse to get her into his truck.

On the road, she was silent for a few minutes before she said anything. "They all seem so… comfortable together."

"The couples?" He saw her nod. "They've been together a while. They're building lives together, even if Naomi won't admit it. Noah and Angelica will get married eventually. They're going to have kids. He's a white picket fence kind of guy."

"Do you want kids?" She quickly covered her mouth with her hand. "You don't have to answer that."

"Jess. Did you miss the part where I said I love you, or the bit where we were talking about planning our future together?"

She shook her head. "I know, but—"

"I *do* want them," he said. "Eventually." He wasn't ready yet. He needed to call Noah's therapist and settle in for some hard work on himself. "Do you?"

She nodded, and he caught a glimmer that might be the sheen of tears in her eyes. "I always have. I just… my family doesn't have a great track record when it comes to making the nuclear family thing work."

"I want to try that with you," he said. "Wow, that sounds really intense when I say it out loud. Don't freak out."

She laughed. "I'm not freaking out. I feel the same way. But you might want to meet my family before you decide."

"Too late for that." He took her hand. "I'm in this for good. Bring 'em on."

"Oh, you're going to need a good night's sleep first," she said.

"Well, then I guess we won't be meeting them tomorrow."

"Why?"

He grinned at her as he pulled the truck into her driveway. "Because I intend to keep you up all night."

"An eco resort?" Sean protested as he was led toward the front desk. "Come on, Jess, do I seem like an eco kind of guy to you?"

His girlfriend grinned. "All natural, all the way, baby."

He snorted, but let her tug him to the desk to check in.

"Casillas-Moore," Jess said to the girl behind the desk.

The girl typed the name in without looking at the keyboard, then paused, her eyes widening as she looked at the screen. "Jessica Casillas-Moore?" When Jess nodded, the girl beamed at her. "I love your show. I stream it every week."

"No cable here?" Sean asked as his eyes bounced around the rustic lobby.

The girl shook her head. "We do have high-speed internet and complimentary WiFi, though. Some people find that their best wellness comes from disconnecting—at least a little bit."

"They can't stop checking their email in between smoothies?" Sean asked. He'd known people like that back in L.A. They preached about living their best lives or being in touch with nature, but their phones were practically glued to their fingers like an extension of their bodies. Hell, he'd been one of them. But unlike him, they'd also carried around their yoga mats like security blankets. Strangely enough, most of their "wellness" routines had been a combination of starvation, nicotine, or cocaine while their Instagram feeds showed a life others tried to emulate. He'd pass.

Jess elbowed him. "Behave," she whispered under her breath.

"Sorry," he said to the girl.

She lifted her shoulders in a small shrug. "You're not entirely wrong." She passed Jess their keys. "Anyway. Welcome to Costa Rica. Since you haven't stayed with us before, let me give you an overview." She pointed, bracelets jangling. "Sauna is over there, and the fitness center is behind it. You've got the therapy pool next to the salt cave, and the leisure pool overlooks the beach." She glanced at the screen. "You're in cabin fourteen, on the beach. Head down the path behind this building to get there. This is an all-inclusive resort, so all of your meals on the property are included. Since this is an alcohol-free resort, all our fresh juices, coffees, and flavored waters are also included."

When the last part of her statement registered, Sean's jaw dropped. He transferred his shocked gaze to Jess, who simply smiled at him. He was pretty sure he could see an actual halo gleaming over her head. "I love you. You know that, right?" He pulled her towards him and kissed her thoroughly. Nobody would be asking him if he wanted a drink. Nobody would be partying a little too hard. Nobody would be setting his nerves on edge with drunken laughter. He felt his entire body relaxing. "Hot damn, now *this* is a vacation."

The front desk attendant smiled at him. "Some guests have the opposite reaction."

"They're probably not recovering alcoholics," he said

blandly as he took the keys out of her hand and set a palm to the small of Jess's back to escort her to their cabin.

Spending New Year's Eve at a luxury resort— alcohol-free!—was definitely one of Jess's better ideas, he decided later as he relaxed in the huge bed while she showered. They'd been together for a few months now, and they'd managed to navigate the fraught possibilities of the holidays with their respective families, as well as their friends.

They'd all bundled into Jess's grandparents' house for Thanksgiving, where Sean had sustained glares from her two brothers and a lot of eye-rolling from her sister. The food had been amazing, though.

At Christmas, they'd agreed to spend the holiday itself apart. Jess had delivered a mountain of gifts to her nephews, some of which he'd helped her pick out. After all, he had a lot of experience being a twelve-year-old boy. Her, not so much. He'd enjoyed the day with his mother, who'd taught him to cook a few of the recipes she'd made for their family on special occasions when he was a kid.

Sean and Jess had spent Christmas Eve together, though, just the two of them. If Santa had come down the chimney at Jess's house that night, he would have been awfully surprised at what was going on under the tree.

The day after Christmas, Noah and Angelica had hosted what Sean suspected was going to become an annual tradition—a lazy afternoon and dinner at The Oakwell Inn, Angelica's B&B. Noah had supplied the wine (for everyone but Sean and Jess, of course), and Max had supplied the food, courtesy of his restaurant, Frankie's. Sean, of course, had brought dessert—he'd worked with Iain and Maeve Brennan, the Irish siblings who owned the local distillery, to make a special whiskey glaze for the cake he'd baked with spices he'd borrowed from Jess's abuela's kitchen. It had been a glorious afternoon. And at the end of it, Jess had surprised him with tickets to this fancy resort in Costa Rica.

"My boss gave me a bit of a bonus," she'd said. "Apparently, advertising on the show is selling exceptionally well. It turns out high-end beauty brands will pay through the nose to reach our audience." She'd beamed at him, pride over her success suffusing her features.

Of course, Sean knew much of the show's success was down to Jess herself, but *she'd* never say it. She might have won more pageants than he could count and have millions of followers on her popular beauty blog, but there wasn't an arrogant bone in her body.

"I guess this means you're not coming to the New Year's Eve party at Frankie's," Max had said.

"It's not like I would have been drinking the champagne," Sean told him pointedly. While he was a lot more open about his struggle with alcohol, thanks in no small part to nearly four months of therapy, he knew parties weren't a great scene for him these days. So did Jess. Which was why she'd come up with a different plan.

Naomi Klein had looked at the brochure Jess had passed around and nodded. "I know this place. They bought one of my pieces at Z Gallery."

"Not the one—" Iain started, but Naomi held up her hand.

"No, not that one. I told you, that one won't ever be up for sale." The artist and the distiller exchanged a private, heated smile.

"Well, I think it sounds great," Angelica said. She paused, looking thoughtful. "I wonder if they've done any renovations lately. We haven't filmed any resorts yet." The former actress shared an agent with Jess, and her popular show on RenoTV featured interesting renovations similar to the one she'd done on her own B&B a couple of years before.

Jess laughed. "I think they're past the point of being

filmed, but if I see any improvements they could make, I'll be sure to pass along your info."

Noah snorted. "That's one filming trip I'll be coming along on."

"You could even have a destination wedding there," Naomi teased. Noah and Angelica's long-delayed wedding was fast becoming a local legend.

The room broke into laughter, and Sean sat back to enjoy the warmth of friendship surrounding him.

Four days later, they'd touched down in Costa Rica, and Sean discovered the true lengths Jess had gone to book the perfect vacation. Now, he peeked at the clock and saw that he had just enough time before dinner to join her in the shower. And if they missed dinner, well, there was always room service.

* * *

THE NEXT EVENING, the resort hosted a New Year's Eve celebration where guests mingled among trays of hors d'oeuvres topped by house-grown microgreens—plus at least twelve different juice concoctions that Sean could spot. He tasted as many as he could.

"We should get a juicer," he said to Jess. He'd finally moved in to her house last month. He liked to joke that it was her kitchen that had won him over; getting to see her every day was just a bonus. The truth was, living in Jess's adorable cottage was a far cry from his bachelor apartment over his mother's garage ... or his high-rise condo back in Beverly Hills. His vintage truck, Bessie Blue, made an idyllic picture parked in front of the sparkling white front porch that she decorated with flower boxes and glass wind chimes. Inside, Jess's taste meshed with his own so well that virtually all he'd brought with him was his beloved mixer. Now they had two. He used both frequently to test new recipes for the bakery.

"Which one do you like the best?" Jess asked. "This carrot and lime one with turmeric is really good."

"This one that looks like a tequila sunrise but is actually beet juice with orange and ginger." He handed her the little shooter glass.

She took a sip and nodded. "We need the recipe."

He chuckled. "Let's see if we can charm it out of somebody."

They wended their way through the crowd hand-in-hand, exchanging greetings with a few couples they'd met at dinner last night and by the pool earlier in the day. Most of the staff they encountered were waiters, passing trays of appetizers and drinks. One of them pointed out the lady in charge, and Sean towed Jess over so they could introduce themselves.

As it happened, not only was Myra Cortone a fan of Jess's show, she'd also heard of River Hill. "I love Angelica Travis," she exclaimed. "Don't tell me you know her!"

Jess smiled. "We do, actually. She's a friend of ours."

"Oh! I wish her show had been around when we did the renovations on this place," Myra remarked.

"Funny that. She said something similar when we told her we were coming here," Jess murmured as Sean suppressed laughter. Clearly Angelica had a kindred spirit in Costa Rica. He looked forward to telling Noah all about it.

"These drinks are so delicious," he told Myra. "Any chance we could get the recipe for a few of them?" He lowered his voice as he asked, in case it wasn't allowed.

She chuckled. "No need to be furtive! We have recipe cards available to all of the guests so that you can make our mocktails at home. We welcome you to take one so that you can transition your organic experience here back into your own lifestyle." She pointed to a little wooden podium nearby. "There's a few baskets of them in the pulpit, if you want to snag them early. They'll be handed out at the door after midnight as part of the thank-you gift for coming, though."

"Pulpit?" Sean's curiosity got the better of him.

"Yes, we frequently host weddings and other private events. We even have a judge on call to conduct ceremonies." She gave them a twinkling smile. "He's also doubles as our tennis instructor."

They laughed, and she bid them farewell to circulate among the other guests. Sean found himself staring at the little podium tucked away at the side of the open-air room, unused for the evening. He let himself picture standing in front of it with Jess, holding hands. Then he pictured waking up next to her the following morning, and every morning after that. He *wanted* it, with every fiber of his being. He glanced at Jess, who was smiling as she watched another couple whirl by in time with the music. He reached out to take her hand, letting his fingers slide along her smooth skin before intertwining them with hers. She looked up at him, and suddenly, everything crystallized.

Sean felt the words rising up in him, and paused only a brief moment to analyze whether he wanted to say them now, or later. No, definitely now. They felt good. It felt *right*. "Jess. Will you marry me? Here? Tomorrow?"

* * *

JESS STARED UP AT SEAN, her jaw slack. Had she heard correctly? *He wanted to marry her? And he wanted it to happen tomorrow?*

"Jess?"

"Yeah?" she whispered weakly. Frankly, she was dumbstruck. It was a miracle she could speak at all.

"Did you hear what I asked?"

Jess nodded mutely.

"And?" The look of hope, love, and contentedness in his eyes was the most profoundly beautiful thing Jess had ever witnessed. Especially considering that the first time she'd seen him all those months ago, his gaze had been hollow and broken. *That* man was a pale shadow of the one standing before her now.

She stepped close and laid her palm against Sean's cheek. He nuzzled into it, his whiskers bristling against her skin. As part of his recovery—he was getting ongoing treatment for both his drinking and the PTSD he'd suffered at finding Cal Grissom's dead body—he'd taken to shaving every morning. It was one small thing, his therapist had explained, that he could do at the start of each day to feel more in control of the world.

Over the holidays, however, he'd relaxed his fastidious grooming habits. The short beard he'd grown was a *choice*; not something that had sprouted up on his face because he couldn't be bothered to do anything about it. They both knew he wasn't one hundred percent healed, but *this* Sean was miles from the man she'd first met.

She loved him. With every fiber of her being, she cherished him.

Jess wanted to be his wife. And she wanted to spend the rest of her days showing him just how far that love extended. If that meant marrying him tomorrow, then that was what she was going to do.

"Yes, I'll marry you!" A surge of happiness so strong and so powerful that it nearly burst right out of her chest welled within her. She laughed, her whole body suffused with joy, and threw her arms around his neck. She jumped into his arms, winding her legs around his waist. He caught her effortlessly, his strong hands molded to her curves. "Yes, yes, yes." She kissed him between each declaration.

Dimly, she became aware they had an audience who were clapping and cheering in the background.

She didn't care. She kept on kissing him all the way back to their cabin.

* * *

"YOUR FAMILY IS GOING to kill me," Sean mused, his fingers tracing a lazy path over her bare skin.

"Mmm-hmm." It was no use pretending otherwise. Her brothers were going to be *pissed*, and Marisol, no doubt, was going to throw a fit. She just hoped her grandparents would forgive her for eloping.

She hadn't been one of those little girls who'd spent countless hours dreaming up the perfect wedding. She'd worn plenty of big, poofy dresses and tiaras over the years, but she'd never really thought of them in terms of being a *bride*.

She *had* always assumed, however, that if and when she got married, her grandfather would give her away. Instead, she'd given *herself* away, meeting Sean halfway down the aisle where they'd walked hand-in-hand to the lush circle of flowers set out on the sandy beach for their ceremony. She'd missed her papa, but it had felt so right to stand tall and meet Sean on her own terms.

That had been three hours ago.

She was a married woman now. In the back of her mind, she tried her new name on for size. *Jessica Amory. Mrs. Sean Amory.* Okay, so it wasn't her name yet. If she wanted to take Sean's last name—and the jury was still out on that, at least professionally—then she'd have a mountain of paperwork to fill out when they got back to the U.S. Otherwise, everything else about their wedding had been pretty straightforward. Easy and breezy (literally), but no less special for its suddenness.

"Is your mom going to be mad?" she asked, pushing up onto her elbows and staring down into his smiling face. They were discussing the possibility of familial rifts they might never recover from, but neither of them could wipe the look of pure and unadulterated happiness from their faces.

Sean shook his head, his smile lazy and warm. "No. She'll be happy for us. You're the daughter she never had. You should prepare yourself to eat a whole lot of cake. " He playfully swatted her naked rear, a little bit softer and rounder than it'd been a few months ago.

Sean wasn't the only one who'd changed. While Jess still exercised several times a week, she wasn't quite as religious about it as she'd once been. These days, if she saw something she wanted to eat, she ate it—including helping Sean taste-test new recipes he was developing for the bakery. A whole new world had opened up to her, but it hadn't been easy.

As part of Sean's therapy program, they'd had a few sessions together. Jess had been surprised when his therapist had requested she join one of their appointments, but within minutes, she'd understood why. By the time she and Sean had walked out an hour later, Jess had the card for a therapist of her own. Jess's sessions weren't scheduled as regularly as Sean's were, but they'd done wonders in helping her come to grips with some very real—and very ugly—truths about her relationship with food and how she used exercise as a coping mechanism. She wouldn't go so far as to say she'd had an eating disorder, but the truth was, she hadn't been far off.

A topic she'd chosen to discuss publicly on her show. The leverage her personal brand afforded her had made it easy for the producers to support her desires. Much like on that long-ago morning show segment with Sylvia Barrows, opening up about the reality of her world and how women were pressured to be perfect—perfect girlfriends, perfect employees, perfect moms—had earned Jess high praise. Not to mention an influx of new viewers. Naturally, the network had been thrilled.

Not so thrilling, however, was donating her old clothes when she'd grown out of them. And she couldn't lie; she'd been worried about how Sean would react to the changes in her body.

Oh, he'd reacted all right.

He couldn't seem to keep his hands off her—not that he'd ever been shy in that regard. But there was something *extra* about the way he loved her these days. He seemed particularly fond of her breasts as they filled up his entire palm.

She dropped a quick kiss onto his nose. "As long as you're prepared for my brothers to behave like assholes, then we're golden."

Sean raised an eyebrow.

"Okay, behave even *more* like assholes."

She giggled, and he pulled her down for a long, slow drugging kiss. "No more talk of your brothers."

* * *

"You didn't!" Angelica gaped at the diamond sparkling atop Jess's left ring finger.

"We did," Sean said with an enormous grin as he tucked Jess into his side.

They were standing in Noah and Angelica's foyer, the last to arrive for their welcome home dinner. They would have been there sooner, but when Sean had added the beautiful Amory family heirloom to the simple platinum bands they'd exchanged in Costa Rica, the time had gotten away from them. The only reason they'd remembered dinner at all was the constant buzzing from the text messages their friends had sent wanting to know where they were.

Angelica's eyes flicked back to Jess's, and if she wasn't mistaken, her friend's gaze turned longing. In a flash though, it was gone. "I'm so happy for you guys."

"Thanks," Jess said with a beaming smile that she was sure matched her husband's.

Her husband.

She'd never get tired of saying that. She still couldn't believe it was true.

Neither could her family.

She and Sean had returned two days ago, and as predicted, things had *not* gone well when they'd shared news of their surprise wedding.

For all of his machismo, she'd never seen her brother Robert lift a hand against anyone, but the second he'd spied the ring on Jess's finger, he'd taken a swing at her new husband. Sean, thankfully, had dodged the flying fist. It turned out his exercise of choice these days was sparring. After forcefully restraining him, Manny and her grandfather had dragged Robert from the room, her two brothers cursing the entire way. With a parting glare, Manny had said that she'd made the biggest mistake of her life. While her grandfather and middle brother were busy dealing with Robert, Marisol had begun to sob noisily. When their abuela had asked why she was crying, Marisol had accused Jess of stealing her thunder. It turned out that she was pregnant again, and had planned on announcing it that night.

Marisol had been easily soothed by the promise of being a consultant for pregnancy-related beauty tips on Jess's show in the spring, something she'd wanted to ask her sister to do anyway. Robert and Manny were less bribe-able, and both left without speaking another word to the newlyweds.

Once all of her siblings had gone home, she and Sean had sat down to a tense dinner with her grandparents. They'd said all the right things, but Jess could tell they remained concerned. By the end of the meal, Sean had managed to charm them at least a little bit—they'd parted with what seemed like genuine smiles and well-wishes, though their moods remained subdued. Jess hoped they would come around..

At least her friends were excited, though.

"I wanna see," Naomi said, hip-checking Angelica out of the way and grabbing hold of Jess's hand. Lifting it to the light for closer inspection, she hummed out her approval. "Mmm, very nice."

Noah chuckled and clapped Sean on the shoulder. To Naomi, he said, "For someone who claims she'll never get married, you sound awfully covetous of a *wedding* ring."

Iain snorted, and when Naomi glared at him, he covered his mouth and turned his head away. Unfortunately, that did nothing to disguise shoulders shaking with laughter.

Naomi rolled her eyes. "There is no *claiming*. We aren't getting married. Such a shame too, since I do love the jewelry."

Iain wrapped his arm around her shoulder and kissed her cheek. "I could buy you a ring," he remarked offhandedly, and all eyes swung his way.

Naomi turned to Iain, her face a mask of surprised wonder mixed with faint suspicion. "You could?" Her throat visibly bobbed as she swallowed deeply.

Iain took hold of Naomi's hand and rubbed the pad of his thumbs lazily over her knuckles. "Sure, I could. It'll be a 'we're going to spend the rest of our lives together living in sin' ring. I hear they're all the rage." He smirked, and Naomi beamed at him.

After a few seconds, she glanced down at Jess's ring. "I do

love diamonds." She paused. "Emeralds, too. And sapphires." Her voice had become dreamy.

Iain chuckled and lifted his chin toward Noah. "I'm gonna need the name of your jeweler. This one isn't lying when she says she loves diamonds. She wouldn't stop talking about Angelica's ring when you proposed."

Noah's eyes found Angelica, who was standing across the circle from him. "How about I take you there myself?" He was speaking to Iain, but his eyes never strayed from his fiancee. "Maybe I'll pick out some wedding rings while I'm at it."

Much as they'd done with Iain's pronouncement, all eyes swung to Noah.

And then to Angelica. For a few brief seconds, she didn't react. But then her gaze grew misty and she nodded. "Yeah, I think it's time we make this official."

By the time Noah broke out a couple of bottles of sparkling grape juice—something he'd been working on in secret for when Sean and Jess came over—there wasn't a dry eye in the house. And if anyone else noticed Max and Maeve's heads bent together, no one said a word.

NOW AVAILABLE: THE BARISTA'S BELOVED

THE BARISTA'S BELOVED
(River Hill #4)

Return to River Hill, where the coffee isn't the only thing that'll leave you buzzing.

It's been months since whiskey maker Maeve Brennan has been on a date, and she's coming dangerously close to giving up on men altogether—until she crosses paths with River Hill's sexy new barista. But Ben's made it clear he only wants to be friends, so Maeve will definitely stop fantasizing about his forearms. Probably. Maybe.

Former lawyer Ben Worthington never thought he'd be living above his best friend's garage and slinging coffee, but there's a lot about his life that doesn't make sense. Like his attraction to the town's beloved distiller. But since Maeve's made it clear she doesn't have time for romance, Ben will stop dreaming about her naked. Soon. Eventually.

But when the youth center where Maeve volunteers comes under fire from a big-city developer, Ben realizes he's the man she needs. He just hopes she can live with his take-no-prisoners approach to winning, because he's pretty sure he can't live without her.

* * *

Chapter One

"To the last two standing!" Maeve Brennan was drunk. She must be, or she wouldn't have toasted her single-hood quite so exuberantly. Max Vergaras clinked glasses with her over the bar, but she didn't miss the wince that crossed his handsome face. She leveled a finger at him. Tried to, anyway. It wove and bobbed until it landed just to the left of his nose, poking into his cheek. "You're not any happier about it than I am."

He gently grasped her finger and removed it from his face. "Not particularly, no."

"Well, what are you doing about it?" Maeve attempted her best intimidating face. She'd grown up with three older brothers who she'd had to hold her own against, so she

208

thought she was doing a pretty good job of it, but Max didn't seem very intimidated.

He shrugged. "It's hard for chefs to date since we have such weird schedules."

Maeve snorted. "So do bakers. And Sean and Jess just got married." Her voice trailed away on the last word. Jessica Casillas-Moore was Maeve's best friend in River Hill, her new hometown. Maeve had moved here with her brother to open up a distillery, far away from their family and the grand whiskey traditions that had ruled them for generations. She'd met Jess when the beauty blogger had started dating a friend of Iain's, and the two had hit it off immediately.

Two days ago, Jess had come back from a surprise trip to Costa Rica with an even bigger surprise: she and Sean had eloped! Which was why Maeve was huddled here at the bar at Frankie's, Max's award-winning restaurant. Ostensibly, she'd come to discuss the joint gift they were planning for the newlyweds. In reality, she'd come to drink.

"Letsh … let's make a pact," she said. "If neither of us is married by the time we're thirty—"

"I'm thirty-five," he said dryly.

"Ugh." She shook her head slowly. "I always forget how old you are."

He rolled his eyes. "Thanks a lot, spring chicken. You should probably dry out." He poured her a glass of water and walked away to go help his staff prepare for the dinner rush.

It was good advice from a wise elder. She didn't take it, though.

Which was why, the next morning, she limped into The Hollow Bean, River Hill's best coffee shop, and ordered her coffee without even looking up over the rim of her oversized sunglasses. The sound of her own voice made her head hurt. Listening to other people was even worse. But nobody had started up a coffee delivery service here yet. She was on her own, and she had a lot to do at work today.

"Here you go." The voice sounded like sunshine. It was the first thing that hadn't set her head to pounding all morning. This time she did look up, and beheld the most beautiful man she'd ever seen. Warm brown eyes circled by thick lashes over an elegant nose that led to a square jaw dusted by a bit of stubble that somehow looked soft. It was like Captain America had personally showed up to make her drink—especially when her eyes darted downward to his chest and her gaze followed his arm as it reached out toward her. He was holding her coffee, the second most beautiful thing in her field of vision.

"Thanks," she managed to get out. Her voice barely made it beyond a rough whisper.

"Rough night, huh?" He smiled, and she was almost certain a breeze ruffled his perfect golden-brown hair. She resisted the urge to look behind her for an assistant with a fan. She wasn't on a reality show. That she knew of, anyway.

"You have no idea," she mumbled.

"Well, enjoy." He turned back to serve other customers, and she spared a moment to watch him walk away. His back was even better than his front, the little coffee shop apron strings cinching around his waist and letting his ass take center stage. It was mesmerizing. But she didn't have time to be mesmerized.

She shuffled back toward the edge of the crowded shop, out of the way, and took her first sip, ready to savor the caffeine-tinged goodness.

It. Was. Awful.

She grabbed for a napkin and wiped her face, sure the vile brew was dribbling down her chin. Raising the cup to eye level, she stared in horror at what had once been her most reliable companion. The cup looked the same—cream cardboard, tan liner, both emblazoned with The Hollow Bean's logo. But what lurked within ...

Maeve sniffed the opening in the lid and recoiled. Whatever this was, it couldn't be called coffee.

She glanced up at the counter and bit her lip. There were three baristas working today—the morning rush was always busy. She hated conflict, but she *needed* coffee.

She watched the line move for a moment. The Hollow Bean was tucked into a tiny building in River Hill's town square in a space clearly not intended to house a coffee shop. Max had said he thought it might once have been an insurance sales office. Now, the baristas were tucked behind a slim counter, sailing around each other in a complicated coffee-making dance that was almost elegant. On the other side of the long swath of burnished marble, things were a lot less pretty. The line curved and bent its way through the space, surrounding the few tiny tables in the front area near the large glass windows. Only the bravest customers actually tried to sit down here, and Maeve wasn't one of them.

Now she carefully edged her way through the crowd to the corner of the counter, out of the way of the people shouting out their orders. The man handing over his credit card at the front of the line shot her a dirty look. She held up her cup in silent self-defense and he rolled his eyes.

It was almost enough to make her back up and leave. She'd had enough conflict in her life—anyone who'd grown up with Cathal Brennan as a father had far more experience with it than they wanted. But where her brothers had grown up into blustery versions of their father—Iain, for the most part, was the exception, though even he could bristle with the best of them—Maeve had decided to just...be nice. She'd discovered a long time ago that people were far more inclined to do what you wanted when you smiled at them than they were when you yelled, and she'd made such a habit of being sweet and accommodating that it had become ingrained. When she'd mustered the courage to tell her family that she and Iain were moving to California, she'd thrown up both before and after the conversation.

But a whiff of the toxic brew in her cup was stronger than the faint nausea the idea of complaining roused in her. She couldn't live without coffee, and she was already too late for work to go anywhere else. She caught the eye of one of the other baristas as he stepped nearby to pour beans into the grinder.

"Excuse me." She raised her cup and put on her best apologetic face. "I'm really sorry, but could I possibly get a fresh one of these?"

He reached out an arm and snagged it with one hand while pushing buttons on the bulky metal machine with the other. He raised it to his nose and sniffed, then sighed. "Ben make this?"

"Uh, the new guy?" She recognized the other two baristas as regulars, but she'd never seen the one who'd made her coffee before. "Yeah."

"You're the third one this morning." The other barista tossed her cup in a bin under the counter. "New guy's hit or miss. He might not work out."

Her jaw dropped. Captain America might get *fired* because she'd complained about her coffee? This was far worse than she'd imagined. She felt her stomach clenching. "Oh, don't- don't do that," she said awkwardly. "He'll get better."

The other man snorted. "We'll see. What'd you have?"

"Er, just a hazelnut latte."

He nodded, and grabbed a fresh cup from the stack. "Give me a minute." Then, to her horror, he turned. "Hey, Ben, come here!"

Maeve looked wildly around. Surely there was a rapidly

opening sinkhole nearby she could leap into. No such natural disaster presented itself, and she came face-to-face with the handsome new guy once again, hoping he didn't notice that her face was rapidly reddening to match the tint of her hair. He gave her a quick smile before turning to the other barista, as though she hadn't just put his entire livelihood on the line. Her imagination was quickly providing her with images of him destitute. The stubble he currently sported would probably grow into a really attractive beard. Maybe he had a pet! It would starve! What had she done?

"Gotta remake the hazelnut latte," the other barista said, completely unaware that there was a hapless dog/cat/bunny/hamster in dire straits.

"Oh, damn," Captain America said. No, Ben. His name was Ben. "Sorry." He turned to Maeve to apologize as well. "Sorry, it's my first day." He gave her a small smile.

She held in a small moan. She was going to get a man and his dog and/or hamster fired on his first day at work, all because she couldn't hold her alcohol.

"Here," the first barista was saying. "I think you forgot to release the valve on the roaster."

"Got it." Ben watched carefully as his fellow barista swiftly prepared Maeve's drink. "Yeah, that's the only thing I did differently. Won't happen again." He took the cup and capped it, scrawling an M on it with the nearby marker. "Maeve, right?"

He pronounced it right, which was a surprise. Most people butchered Irish names. "Yeah."

"Here you go. Really sorry about that."

She reached out to take the coffee, and his fingers brushed hers as he let go. She shivered. He noticed. His smile edged sideways a little and his eyes warmed further. She could feel herself getting even redder. "Um. Thanks. Sorry for, uh, the inconvenience."

He held up a hand. "Don't apologize! You needed a new cup. I did it wrong."

She glanced at the other barista, who'd already hurried off to take care of another customer. "But if something happens—"

He chuckled. "I'm not going to lose my job over one poorly made coffee."

"He said it was three," she blurted without thinking. She didn't want him to lose his job, but surely he needed to be aware that it was a possibility. Something Jess had said the other day drifted through her mind. *Oh, for the confidence of a mediocre white man.* Charming was one thing. Entitled was another. She pressed her lips together to avoid saying anything more out loud, though.

"Every one a learning experience," Ben said. He aimed what was clearly intended to be a devastating smile at her.

She raised her eyebrows and lifted her coffee to her nose, taking a tentative sniff before she sipped. She let out a small, satisfied sigh as the warm liquid filtered through her. She looked up to see Ben still watching her, his lips parted slightly. "Thanks. I'll get out of your way now." She stepped back, and he visibly shook himself.

"It was nice to meet you, Maeve," he said. "Next time you come in, coffee's on me."

She laughed. "Who's making it?"

"Ouch." He chuckled. "Enjoy your day."

She slid away from the counter as he turned to catch the cup being handed to him by one of the other baristas. A few more sips of coffee as she headed out the door, and her hangover was definitely on the downswing.

A few minutes later, she pulled into the parking lot of Whitman's Distillery feeling significantly better than she had at the start of the day. Good coffee and and even better eye candy went a long way to easing the shock of your best friend getting married.

Not that she wasn't happy for Sean and Jess. She was just … she didn't know what, exactly, but it felt a lot like lonely.

It might not amount to anything, but suddenly Maeve thought she might take Captain America up on his offer of coffee sometime. If nothing else, he was certainly pretty to look at.

ABOUT THE AUTHORS

Rebecca Norinne and Jamaila Brinkley have been friends for almost fifteen years. Separately, they write contemporary romance and historical fantasy romance; together, they created the enchanting world of River Hill. In this charming Northern California town, Norinne and Brinkley combined the interests that made them friends in the first place—great food, delicious wine, and a pinch of home renovation—and added in the spicy romance they love.

Rebecca lives in Massachusetts with her husband, and Jamaila lives in Maryland with her husband and twin children. They email each other a lot.

9 780999 822541